"She told me you didn't love me."

Verity shrugged. "I was aware of that, of course, and that you would always love her, would presumably carry on—I use the term deliberately—as you'd always done." She winced as Ben's fingers gripped her arms through the thin sleeves.

"And you believed every word," he said harshly. Verity stared at him, her head thrown back in defiance.

"She was so convincing, Ben. Especially the Parthian shot she let fly as an exit line." A shudder of distaste ran through her body. "She's pregnant, she told me, and Peter's on cloud nine. Unfortunately for him Gussie implied the child was more likely to be yours. Could it be yours, Ben...could it?"

Desirable Property

Catherine George

Harlequin Books

TORONTO • NEW YORK • LONDON
AMSTERDAM • PARIS • SYDNEY • HAMBURG
STOCKHOLM • ATHENS • TOKYO • MILAN

Original hardcover edition published in 1984
by Mills & Boon Limited

ISBN 0-373-02720-6

Harlequin Romance first edition October 1985

CHAPTER ONE

IN the distance a church clock struck three. The chimes hung on the warm, still air as Verity stopped the car, her eyes lingering with delight on the view. From the layby at the foot of the steep hill the village of Priorsford could be seen in its entirety, the houses of honey-coloured stone, their steeply pitched roofs sharply defined against the blue sky, climbing up the main street in the hot July sunlight, giving way to the Bell Inn in pride of place at the top. For a few tranquil moments she sat still, just gazing, then at last she surrendered to the compulsion that drew her like a magnet, and turned her head to look in the opposite direction, where Tern Cottage laid sole claim to the attention.

It stood some distance away below the village, on a small mound encircled by one of the tributaries of the River Avon; a miniature castle complete with moat, a narrow rustic bridge in place of drawbridge giving access to the path that wound sharply upwards through a garden tiered with beds of roses and flowering shrubs. Verity drew in a deep breath, ruefully aware that every time she laid eyes on the house she coveted it with an intensity that broke the tenth commandment.

On the car seat beside her lay clip-board, leather-cased steel tape, camera and briefcase in readiness for her appointment at Tern Cottage. Acquainted with her client of old Verity knew very well it would be a waste of time to arrive early, and got out to while away the time with her camera, taking several shots of the house and garden from below before returning to the car to run a comb through her heavy brown hair, retying the ribbon securing it at the nape of her neck. As she inspected her face in the driving mirror her attention was distracted by the sight of a man descending the twists and turns of the path from the cottage at breakneck speed. Verity watched, her eyebrows raised, wondering idly why anyone should exert themselves so violently in such heat, her hazel eyes bright with interest as the man strode past blindly and vaulted into a dark green sports car parked a few yards away, just beyond a Mercedes convertible. She winced as the engine revved angrily to life and the car roared up the steep village street, shattering the somnolent quiet of the afternoon.

Verity was intrigued. Her fleeting glimpse of the man had been enough for an impression of swarthy skin, tightly curling black hair—and rage; all the more intimidating for its grim suppression. Wondering what had upset the man so badly she gathered up her belongings and locked the car before making her way, at a very much more leisurely pace, up the path the unknown man had just hurtled down so precipitously. Verity hesitated as she reached the house. The heavy, studded door stood open into the dim hall, and after a moment she lifted the iron knocker, in the shape of a lion's head, and let it fall. At once quick footsteps sounded on the staircase inside, and a light, petulant voice called,

'I hope you've come back to apologise!'

The door flew open and Verity was confronted by the lady of the house, dressed in white silk shirt and trousers, silver-gilt hair framing a pretty face marred by red swollen lids over blue eyes that stared blankly at the tall, slender girl standing in the doorway.

'Hello, Gussie. Is this a bad time? You specified three-fifteen to my boss yesterday.' Verity spoke with matter-of-fact friendliness, tactfully ignoring all signs of distress.

'Lord, yes. No, I mean, Verity Marsh, of course. Come in, darling. Sit down somewhere.' Augusta Middleton fluttered her hands vaguely towards what had once been termed the parlour. 'Go into the drawing-room. I'll be with you in a sec, must do something about my face.'

Verity sat on one of the tightly-buttoned pink settees in the drawing-room, looking out through the open latticed windows at the garden at the back of the house; no flower beds here, just a steep slope of lawn from a small paved terrace to the graceful willows fringing the river bank below. The room itself jarred on her. Gussie had ignored its personality, and white furry carpet and pink silk curtains were uneasy companions for the beamed ceiling and the cowled stone fireplace in the inglenook. Verity was openly curious. Gussie had obviously been having quite a stand up fight with her visitor, whoever he was, moreover, Gussie's mouth had been almost as swollen as her eyelids, though presumably for a different reason, and none of the crystal buttons on her silk shirt were thrust through the corresponding buttonholes. None of your business, Verity told herself with a grin, and turned as her hostess came back with newly made-up face and a bright smile of apology.

'Sorry, Verity. A spot of bother just now before you came. I do apologise. Frightfully good of you to come, darling.'

'Not at all; my job,' said Verity.

'I know—so clever of you to be a surveyor, or whatever it is.' Gussie sat on the arm of a chair, one foot in its gilt sandal swinging idly. 'Of course, you always were such a practical sort of girl—too marvellous to be so competent.'

The words were no compliment, but Verity smiled pleasantly, mentally gritting her teeth.

'I do my best, Gussie. Thank you for asking for me specifically. I gather from my boss you insisted on it.'

Gussie jumped up and prowled restlessly around the room.

'I knew you loved the dreary old place. I thought you'd do your best to stress its attractions so it'll sell quickly.'

Verity's eyes narrowed in surprise. 'But I thought Peter's father spent a small fortune in restoring the house, Gussie. I assumed you adored it,' she said slowly.

The other girl's mouth tightened. 'Adore it! I loathe the place. Olde-worlde cottages are for looking at, not living in, I assure you, darling. Besides, it's miles away from anywhere. Who could like being stuck in this God-forsaken hole in winter?'

I, for one, thought Verity.

'Does Peter want to move?' she asked.

Gussie tossed her head with a pitying little smile. 'Peter wants what I want, darling!'

'But it's such a beautiful location——'

'You can't be serious!' Gussie rounded on Verity scornfully. 'It's like living in a goldfish bowl. All the village can see whoever comes and goes—the front garden is open to all eyes. Then there's no garage, the cars have to stay in the layby down below, and we can't even get permission to build one, or tear down that ramshackle bridge, because of some beastly preservation order. When we go out I have to trail down to the car in wellies and with a golf umbrella if it's raining, and if I'm very tired when we come home Peter just has to carry me up to the house!'

Remembering Peter's tendency to overweight Verity thought privately a move might be his only chance of survival if he was obliged to hoist his rather voluptuously built wife up the path every night. Keeping her face straight with an effort she took out her pen and armed herself with her clipboard and tape.

'It might be a good idea to keep your opinions quiet when people come to view the house, Gussie. The idea is to stress the good points, you know. Now, perhaps I'd better get started. Peter's out, I take it—I rather hoped he might be here to help me measure up. No one else from the firm was free to come with me as it's Saturday afternoon.'

Gussie had the grace to look a little guilty. 'Horrors, Verity—I never thought. I suppose you don't normally work on Saturday afternoon. I *am* sorry.'

'Not to worry,' said Verity lightly. 'The offices are open on Saturdays, and even Sunday mornings at the height of the season. This just happened to be my weekend off.'

'You should have said something, darling——'

Verity laughed. 'When my boss tells me to jump, Gussie, believe me, I jump! Besides it won't take long, then I can return to my own back lawn and sunbathe.'

Gussie's face fell. 'But I thought you'd at least stay to tea, Verity. Peter's away for the weekend on some beastly course, Mummy and Daddy are on holiday, and I'm all alone. Please! We can have it on the terrace in the sun, and Mrs Dutton, my woman, made a super cake yesterday.'

She looked so like a sulky child balked of a treat Verity laughed and gave in, on condition Gussie lent a hand, if only to hold the other end of the tape. The property was certainly desirable, but by no means large. Originally three farm labourers' cottages, it had been converted into one dwelling in the previous century and given the name 'Tern', meaning a set of three, not after the inappropriate sea-bird as generally supposed. The conversion had been brought to its present state of perfection by the efforts of Henry Middleton, a self-made millionaire who was able to hire people with taste and skill to make what he jocularly called a 'love-nest' for his son and his beautiful bride, resulting in what most people would consider a dream house. Besides the spacious hall, which retained one of the original fireplaces, the ground floor offered an unusually large kitchen, with windows looking out on both front and back gardens, a smallish, but pretty dining-room and the drawing-room. Upstairs three bedrooms and two bathrooms, one en suite with the master bedroom, gave on to a landing with a carved wood balustrade running round three sides of the upper floor and overlooking the hall below.

One half of Verity took measurements and made notes with her usual speed and efficiency, while the other half constantly marvelled that any woman in her right senses could give up such a house. Fortunately, Peter Middleton had left a list of helpful details regarding damp course, re-wiring, dry-rot treatment and insulation, confirming Verity's findings, and over tea on the sunlit terrace an hour later she was able to advise a very satisfactory asking price, the house quite definitely at the top of its particular category in the property market.

'Fantastic, Verity!' Gussie's eyes gleamed. 'Now we can look round for something in Stratford, or as near it as possible. Keep an eye out, darling. I fancy something split-level with a swimming-pool, and a really secluded garden. All this boring antiquity leaves me utterly cold. You should hear the creaks and groans in the night! I know it's only the timbers and all that, but it terrifies me when I'm on my own.'

Verity eyed her over her teacup, shaking her head slightly. 'In my opinion it's a beautiful house, Gussie; quite perfect.'

'Exactly, darling, that's why I asked your boss at Lockhart & Welch to make sure you came to do the necessary.' Gussie leaned towards Verity eagerly. 'I say, darling, I don't suppose you'd stay the night? I did have something planned, but it's fallen through, and with Peter away I shall be all alone.'

Verity shook her head. 'Sorry, Gussie. I'm dining Greek with a friend of mine.'

'Man?'

'Yes.' Verity smiled in amusement. 'Though I have been known to spend evenings with other females sometimes.'

Gussie shuddered. 'How deadly!' She hesitated, looking at Verity as she lay stretched out indolently in a garden chair, her face turned up to the sun, bare arms and legs brown against the white of her denim shirt-dress. 'Vee, darling, did you, er, see anyone when you arrived?'

Verity opened an eye. 'If you mean a dark, very irate

gentleman with a tremendous burst of speed, yes. He passed as I was sitting in the car.'

Gussie sighed, her mouth drooping. 'That was Ben Dysart.'

Verity's other eye opened, her interest caught. 'The one you had a crush on when we were in school?'

Gussie nodded glumly. 'That's the one. We had a row this afternoon.'

'I rather gathered that.' Verity's eyes danced. 'That wasn't all you had, I imagine, from the look of you when I arrived. Your shirt buttons are still adrift, by the way.'

Gussie hastily repaired the damage, eyeing Verity uncertainly. Suddenly she burst out—'I have to tell someone, Verity. I'm in such a frightful turmoil.'

Verity held up a hand hastily. 'Now don't tell me anything you'll regret, Gussie—you might be sorry afterwards.'

'I used to tell you things in school,' muttered Gussie, twisting one of her shirt buttons.

'Girlish confidences whispered after lights out in school are a bit different from what I'm afraid you're about to confess now,' said Verity levelly, her hazel eyes very bright and direct. 'That was ten years ago and our lives have diverged since school. You're a socialite and I'm a working girl—remember, I'm here only in a professional capacity this afternoon.'

Great, facile tears began to roll down Gussie's cheeks and she sniffed like a miserable child. Verity sighed and handed her a table napkin.

'Please!' Gussie turned drowned blue eyes on Verity. 'I must tell someone, and with you I know there'll be absolute discretion.'

Verity heard the last word with distaste, glanced at her watch, then said crisply, 'All right, Augusta Middleton. If you must, you must. But in twenty minutes I'm away, no matter what.'

Gussie mopped her eyes and began to talk. 'Ben— Benedict actually—is the son of a baronet.'

Verity frowned. 'Dysart, you said. Didn't someone of that name die in a fire not so long ago?'

Gussie nodded. 'That was Nick, Ben's older brother. There were just the two of them. Of course when Ben and I were, well, involved, Ben was the younger brother, a mere Lieutenant in the Royal Marines. He only had his pay, and just between you and me my parents weren't at all well off after Daddy's business went down the drain, and there was Peter, always on hand.'

'Not in the bush,' murmured Verity.

Gussie ignored her. 'I knew Ben would be a Captain eventually, and all that, but I couldn't face the thought of married quarters, or whatever I should have had to endure as a sort of camp follower, and the Dysarts aren't exactly rolling in cash, it's all land and property, if you follow me.'

'Perfectly.'

'And there was Peter, absolutely potty about me, and with all that lovely money from his father's computers I felt I really had no choice. Oh it's so unfair,' went on Gussie passionately. 'How could I know Nick Dysart would snuff it—now Ben will inherit the title and all the rest of it, but I'm all tied up to Peter. Not that I'm not fond of Peter, of course, but he doesn't turn me on like Ben and——'

'I think I have the picture,' said Verity hurriedly, and got up, feeling it was time to go. She looked at Gussie curiously. 'Would I be vulgarly curious if I asked why you had such a row?'

Gussie stood up, running her hands through her hair. She looked away. 'I rang him up and asked him to come over when I knew Peter would be away. The subject of divorce came up, then he got in an absolute rage and said horrid things when I suggested he stay the night.'

Verity bit her lip as she gathered up her belongings. 'Don't you want to divorce Peter, Gussie?' she asked point blank. 'If you're so hot for this man Dysart I'm sure Peter would let you go.'

Gussie's tears gushed again. 'I *can't* ask for a divorce, Verity.' She sniffed and dabbed at her eyes carefully. 'I said Daddy's business went on the rocks, didn't I? He was in debt and pretty desperate and—and Peter's father bailed him out, but only on condition I stuck by Peter.' She shot Verity an odd, shamefaced look. 'Besides, I'm *fond* of Peter, and I *like* having oodles of money—I might as well be honest. Did you see my Mercedes in the layby? Peter just gave me that for my birthday. I really don't see why Ben couldn't, well, spend a little time with me now and again when it's convenient.'

Verity stared at the pouting loveliness of Gussie's face and shook her head in wonder. 'You quite honestly don't do you—you want the penny *and* the bun.' Belatedly she remembered Gussie was a client. 'Anyway, it's really none of my business, though I can't help a reluctant glimmer of approval for your ex-beau for refusing your tempting offer.'

Gussie's eyes hardened. 'He'll change his mind, never fear. I only have to wait.'

As they left the terrace for the kitchen, a loud, impatient knock sounded on the front door.

'Hang on a minute, Verity. I'll just see who it is.' Gussie hurried into the hall. Verity checked on her belongings then went more slowly after her hostess, standing still in embarrassment as she saw a powerfully built man with somewhat familiar black curly hair grasp Gussie by her shoulder, shaking her as he looked down into her triumphant face.

'All right, you win,' he grated. 'I only got as far as the Bell. I warn you I've had too much to drink, and now the only thing on my mind is your tempting invitation, Mrs Middleton. So I'm back.' He bent his head and kissed Gussie's willing mouth so explicitly Verity coloured to the roots of her hair and prepared to depart as noiselessly as possible to leave the happy pair to it. In her haste she dropped her briefcase and the couple in the hall sprang apart, Gussie's face guilty, the man's hard features cold with anger.

'Sorry,' said Verity calmly. 'Don't mind me, I was just going—thanks for the tea, Gussie.' She ignored the man and smiled at the other girl, who gathered herself together with an effort and did her best to preserve the social niceties.

'Oh Verity, do let me introduce an old friend of mine—Ben Dysart.' She gestured helplessly. 'Ben, this is Verity Marsh. We were in school together.'

'How do you do,' said Verity without expression.

Ben Dysart inclined his head very slightly. 'Miss Marsh,' he said flatly, and stood his ground, very rigid and erect. Even so he failed to tower over Verity, who stood five feet eight in her bare feet and was addicted to high heels. After one brief, disinterested look she ignored him and addressed herself to Gussie.

'I'll set the wheels in motion first thing on Monday. We'll advertise the cottage extensively and send you the paperwork as soon as we have the photographs.'

From the corner of her eye she saw Ben Dysart's eyebrows move a trifle.

'Is Tern Cottage up for sale, Gussie?' he asked quickly.

'Yes, darling—you never gave me a chance to tell you earlier.' Gussie smiled with calculated intimacy at her poker-faced visitor. 'Peter and I want a more modern place nearer town, with more privacy. Don't you think that's a much better idea than living in the sticks like this?'

Ex-Captain Benedict Dysart's air of hot importunity seemed to have evaporated.

'Personally I'm rather attached to "the sticks" as you put it; each one to his own taste, of course,' he said stiffly, and looked at Verity properly for the first time. 'And you, I assume, are going to sell it for her, Miss Marsh?'

'Hopefully, yes.' Verity moved thankfully towards the door. 'Goodbye, then, Gussie. Goodbye, Mr Dysart.' She smiled politely and made her escape, obliged to exert considerable self-control not to bolt down the drive as Ben Dysart had earlier. Not that she expected the happy pair to be watching her, they were more likely to be locked in each other's arms again, if the earlier impassioned embrace had been anything to go by.

Verity drove the eight meandering miles back to Stratford wondering philosophically what it was Gussie had that made men get so primitive. No one had ever smouldered over Verity Marsh in her entire twenty-six years. She sighed, then laughed at herself, not really sorry when she came to consider it. She had a strong suspicion that all that unbridled passion might be a shade embarrassing if channelled in her own direction, as her own response was more likely to be amusement than any answering fire. She had no false modesty about her own attractions. Tall, with a figure more aptly described as athletic rather than voluptuous, she nevertheless curved in and out very nicely in the required places. Her hazel eyes shone through a thick fringe of lashes the same rich brown as her hair, which hung, glossy and slightly curling to her shoulders, and her skin was good, olive-tinted; the type that tanned easily and evenly at the first glimpse of summer sun. Her main drawback, according to one of her numerous men-friends, was her self-sufficiency. He had advised a little helpless femininity now and then, but Verity found this quite beyond her; if something needed doing she did it, and that was that. Heigh-ho, she thought goodhumouredly, the Gussies of this world get doting husbands plus masterful lovers, while I must be content with a circle of pleasant friends of both sexes, who were admittedly showing disturbing signs of pairing up in one way or another of late. Picturing herself as the only one left in single harness she decided the solution was a cat, maybe two, and concentrated on threading her way through a crowded Stratford-upon-Avon, crossing the river bridge in the direction of the home she had been born in and never moved from apart from her years in college.

Verity parked the car in the garage at the side of the solid, pre-war house and went round to the back lawn, where two figures in bikinis lay prone on garden chairs, their faces turned to the sun. They sat up at the sound of her footsteps, one slender and ethereal looking, with long fair hair and blue eyes; Miss Henrietta Carr, aspiring actress, the other girl sturdily built, with reddish curly hair and kind, intelligent brown eyes that looked at Verity in enquiry as the latter cast herself down on the grass, careless of grass-stains on her white dress.

'Hard day, Vee?' Jenny Blair was sympathetic and got up to pour a glass of lemon squash from a thermos on the wrought-iron table.

Verity drank gratefully. 'Thanks, Jenny. I haven't been to the office; just a special visit to a friend's house to measure up and so on.'

Henrietta grinned, stretching. 'Vee's socialite friend, Jen, the upmarket Mrs Middleton—glamorous Gussie. How was she, Verity?'

'Just the same,' said Verity neutrally. 'What time are you due at the theatre, Hett?'

'Ten minutes ago—I'd better be off.'

'What are you tonight?' asked Jenny, settling herself comfortably.

'Singing fairy in *The Dream*.' Henrietta waved a regretful hand and went off to change.

'When are you on duty again, Jenny?' asked Verity.

'Not until Monday.' Jenny looked disgruntled. 'But then I'm on nights for a spell—almost right up to the wedding.' She was a staff-nurse, and engaged to a trainee GP attached to one of the local medical practices.

'Bad luck—never mind. You'll soon be honeymooning in Spain and living happily ever after.'

Jenny looked at Verity's face thoughtfully. 'Do I detect a cynical note, Miss Marsh?'

Verity opened her eyes to smile at the other girl warmly. 'Not as far as you're concerned, love. Richard coming round tonight?'

Jenny nodded.

'A quiet evening *chez moi* is the best we can do at the moment. Saving all the spare pennies for Spain. You don't mind his spending so much time here Verity?'

'Of course not, silly. I'm going out with Neill tonight, Hett is treading the boards as usual—have fun.' Verity looked up with surprise as the budding actress came back wearing a thin cotton dress. 'My goodness, Hett, not often we see you in a dress! Something on tonight?'

'I think so.' Henrietta frowned vaguely. 'One of the musicians suggested a snack, but I can't remember whether he said tonight or tomorrow, so I thought I'd go prepared.' She floated off as the girls laughed goodnaturedly at her.

'I'll miss her when she leaves at the end of the season—you too, Jen, when you're a married lady. The joys of being a landlady!' Verity sighed and sat down on the other chair.

'You'll have no trouble letting two such comfortable bedsits, Verity,' Jenny assured her. 'And you're in the right business for it.'

'I think sometimes I'll sell the house and get a flat myself. I'd hate to hurt my mother's feelings though, after all, it was marvellous of her to make the house over to me when she married Ian, my stepfather.' Verity looked pensive. She felt oddly flat and lethargic, suddenly in no mood for moussaka and bouzouki music with Niall Gordon, who was bound to talk shop all night as he worked for one of the other estate agents in the town.

'Wouldn't you have liked to live with your mother and Ian?' asked Jenny.

'It would have meant giving up my job here and chancing finding another in Birkenhead. Added to which I think newly-weds should be on their own, whatever age they are. My mother had been a widow for a long time—Dad died when I was ten—so I expect she had some adjusting to make to the life of a schoolmaster's wife. A large encumbrance in the shape of a ready-made daughter for Ian would hardly have been a help.' Verity sat up and swung her legs to the ground. 'This way I have company in the house in the shape of you two, the extra money pays the rates and so on, and I stay in my beloved home town. Now get off your trim little behind and come and have some tea.'

The weather broke over the weekend, and a cool drizzle started as Verity was walking to work the following Monday morning, dampening her spirits somewhat by the time she reached the rather imposing offices of Lockhart & Welch. The reception area exuded a tangible atmosphere of prosperity and success, with large coloured photographs of beautiful houses arranged in collages on the panelled walls, the two attractive receptionists seated at mahogany desks facing each other across an expanse of deep-piled crimson carpet. Both girls looked up with a smile as Verity came through the big glass doors shaking the scarf that had covered her hair from the unexpected rain.

'Mr Randall would be pleased if you could spare him a moment before you start, Verity,' said Nicola, the dark one. 'He's already in his office.'

'On my way,' said Verity cheerfully. 'See you, girls.'

She knocked on the door marked 'J. R. Randall' and went in without waiting, sitting down in one of the easy chairs while the gentleman in question finished a telephone conversation. He was a slim man in his early forties, with a narrow, clever face and deceptively sleepy blue eyes beneath receding fair hair. He put down the receiver and smiled at Verity.

'Good morning. How did it go on Saturday at Tern Cottage?'

'Very well.' Verity took her notes from her briefcase. 'As far as I could see not a thing wrong with the place at all, considering its age. Peter Middleton's father had a damp-course installed, wiring renewed, dry rot treated and extra insulation added, the fittings in the kitchen and bathrooms are positively sumptuous, and of course

the garden is beautiful. One snag, though, no garage—
only the layby at the foot of Priorsford Hill.'

'Anywhere to build one?' John Randall reached out a
hand for her notes and studied her clear handwriting.

'Without research into it I'm not sure, but Gussie—
Mrs Middleton—says there's some preservation order
preventing it.' Verity shrugged. 'She's not exactly hyper-
efficient with facts and figures, and Peter Middleton
was away, unfortunately. He left me a list of the salient
points, but he doesn't mention the garage. Do you
think it will detract much from the value of the house?'

'Not necessarily. I see you've put a fairly steep price
on it, so the vendors could afford to come down a bit, if
necessary.' He looked up with a smile. 'I'm glad you
could spare the time to make the trip out there on
Saturday. I'm aware it was your weekend off.'

She looked back at him ruefully.

'Despite all your careful euphemisms, Mr Randall,
sir, i.e. "could you spare a moment", or "if you can
manage it", you know only too well that you whistle
and I come running.'

He chuckled. 'Very right and proper too.' The smile
faded as he regarded her thoughtfully. 'I'm not being
euphemistic when I say I would like a favour of you,
Verity. You are perfectly at liberty to refuse if you
wish.'

Verity stirred uneasily in her chair. 'What do you
want me to do?'

'I have a friend who needs to bone up on estate
management. He's coming to spend a few weeks with
us, more or less sitting in with various people to find
out how we do things. I'd rather like him to start with
you—go out to the various vendors, accompany you on
actual surveys whenever possible, get the feel of things
generally. John Humphries is on holiday, so you're the
next best thing in his absence.'

'Don't overwhelm me with too much flattery,' said
Verity wryly. 'I might ask for a rise.'

'You know perfectly well you're a very bright young

surveyor, regardless of age and sex. John Humphries isn't nearly as pretty, but he's been with the firm ten years longer.' The sleepy blue eyes were openly laughing at her and Verity grinned back, her hackles subsiding.

'O.K. Wheel in your chum whenever you like. In the meantime I'll get on with earning my salary.'

'Thanks, Verity. I'll deliver him into your hands mid-morning sometime.'

Verity's far less sumptuous cubicle was in the modern extension built on to the back of the much older front premises. She took one look at her desk and made an attack on the work waiting for her. In her absorption the time passed unnoticed until the door opened just before eleven and she looked up with a welcoming smile, thinking coffee had arrived. The smile faded. Her face felt stiff with surprise as John Randall ushered Ben Dysart into the room.

CHAPTER TWO

'BEN DYSART, Verity,' said her boss amiably. 'Ben this is Verity Marsh, who has kindly volunteered to give you the benefit of her not inconsiderable expertise. I'll leave you in her capable hands.' He withdrew, closing the door behind him.

'It's very good of you to volunteer as mentor, Miss Marsh.' Ben Dysart's face was inscrutable as he bowed slightly.

'I feel I should point out that the word "volunteer" was Mr Randall's, not mine,' Verity informed him. 'However, I shall do my best to give you any help I can, of course. Do sit down.'

He sat, looking so swarthy and alien in the cramped little room that Verity wondered crossly if some gypsy blood had nourished the Dysart family tree at some stage. This man was the very antithesis of her idea of British aristocracy.

'I realise this must be somewhat embarrassing for you,' he said, his voice hard and clipped. 'I assume you were ignorant of my identity before John wished me on you.'

Verity smiled coolly. 'Yes. But it makes no difference, Mr Dysart. Even if I had any personal feelings in the matter—which I don't—they would hardly interfere with my job. If Mr Randall wants me to give you help I shall do my best to oblige. I do what I'm told.'

'Always?'

Even white teeth showed unexpectedly in a smile that threw her slightly off-balance. She ignored his question and motioned him to bring his chair nearer so that she could make a start on explaining her contribution to the function of Lockhart & Welch, Chartered Surveyors. Her office, never spacious, now seemed minuscule. Not a girl given much to phobias, Verity was gripped by unfamiliar pangs of claustrophobia as her companion sat in enforced proximity, his thigh almost touching her own and his face uncomfortably near as he leaned over her desk. Steadily Verity went on with her explanations, but was never more glad to see the door open and a coffee tray appear, borne in by the other receptionist, Sally, her face bright with interest as she gave an admiring glance at Verity's companion.

'Thank you very much.' Verity smiled at the girl, who withdrew slowly, her eyes lingering on Ben Dysart.

'I didn't think people actually had trays of coffee brought to them any more,' he remarked as he took the cup Verity offered.

'*I* don't, certainly, I normally just get handed a cup. This is VIP treatment because you're here.' She perched on the corner of her desk to drink her coffee, glad to put space between herself and this man who sat so disconcertingly still. It would have been easier if there had been any tranquillity in the stillness, but Verity was put in mind of a tiger about to leap on its quarry. 'Mr Randall dislikes machines, so we get the real thing,' she said for something to say. 'Can I offer you another cup?'

'No thanks.' Ben put his cup back on the tray, then looked her in the eye inexorably. 'I think there's something I should clear up, Miss Marsh, before we go any further. Last Saturday——'

'Please!' Verity slid off the desk, putting her own cup back with a click. 'I'd rather we forgot about last Saturday. It was embarrassing and unfortunate, but absolutely nothing to do with me, Mr Dysart—entirely your own affair, *and* Gussie's.'

Verity's eyes narrowed as they noted the amusement lurking at the corners of Ben Dysart's wide, rather sensuous mouth. 'Very true, Miss Marsh,' he said silkily, 'but not at all what I was going to say. You should avoid putting words in other people's mouths.'

Verity flushed and sat down in her chair with ill-grace, feeling both foolish and resentful. 'I'm sorry,' she said with difficulty.

He inclined his head graciously. 'Last Saturday,' he began again, 'was the first time I had any idea the Middletons intended selling Tern Cottage.'

Verity frowned in surprise. 'Do you know someone who might be interested in purchasing?'

'Yes. Me.' His face was so expressionless Verity thought for a moment she'd misheard.

'I'm sorry? Did you say you?'

'I did.' He crossed his legs and leaned back in his chair, his eyes on her frankly surprised face.

'But I thought——' Verity checked herself and started again. 'As you inherit a title and an estate I wouldn't have thought you needed somewhere to live. Or is the cottage intended for an employee?'

'Yes, me.' He smiled as Verity looked blank. 'Temple Priors only becomes mine on my father's death, which, God willing, will be many years hence. In the meantime, much as I love my parents, naturally I'd very much prefer a place of my own.'

'I see.' Verity thought she saw only too well.

'Presumably you know that my brother died in a fire while my parents were on holiday.' Ben's tone was colourless. 'He was the true expert on the estate, but now I more or less have to dive in at the deep end and take a crash-course in land management, and how to run an estate. The idea is to take over from my father as soon as I can—not entirely, of course, but his health is worrying my mother a bit. From my point of view it's quite a re-adjustment, as most of my adult life has been spent in the Marines in various parts of the globe.'

'Yes. It can't be easy, Mr Dysart, or should it be Captain, or Major?' Verity looked at him in enquiry.

'Neither. I answer to "Ben" quite satisfactorily.'

She went on doodling on her blotter, trying to choose her next words with care. 'As far as Tern Cottage is concerned, what exactly did you have in mind?'

'Nothing underhand, I assure you,' he retorted acidly.

Verity's chin came up, her eyes hostile. 'I made no such suggestion, Mr Dysart.'

'It wasn't necessary. Your eyes made it for you.'

They glared at each other for a moment, then Ben checked himself visibly.

'I apologise,' he said stiffly. 'I merely wanted to say that when Tern Cottage comes officially on the market I shall offer whatever price Peter Middleton is asking for it.'

There was silence in the room for a few moments. 'Does Mrs Middleton know you want the cottage?' asked Verity at last, not looking at him.

'No,' he said shortly. 'In fact my father will make the offer. Our land runs down to the river at the back of the cottage; the purchase will round out the estate and that's all *Gussie*'—he emphasised the name—'will need to know. She will accept it more easily that way.'

'I see.' This was untrue, as Verity knew Gussie was only too eager to get rid of the cottage, and unlikely to care who bought it as long as she could have the more modern, convenient house she wanted. 'Right,' she went on briskly, 'now shall we revert to the subject of surveys, Mr Dysart, or have you had enough for the time being?' Her smile was pleasant, but privately she wished him anywhere but under her aegis to augment his education.

Ben stood up, his breadth of shoulder impressive, even in conservative tweed jacket and correct collar and tie. 'I thought we might have a pub lunch together,' he suggested.

'I think not.' Verity was in much need of a respite. 'I usually just eat a sandwich in the park, thank you.'

He gestured towards the small window. 'It's pouring out there.'

'In which case I shall eat my sandwich right here at my desk,' she said sweetly.

Ben shrugged. 'Just a thought. Some other time perhaps. See you later.'

Verity stared moodily at his straight back as he went through the door, then slumped in her seat, feeling drained. On impulse she picked up the telephone and asked for John Randall.

'Verity,' she said tersely, when he answered. 'Is Mr Dysart with you?'

'No.'

'How long is he to stay with me?' she demanded.

'As long as it takes—at least all this week. That all right with you?' Her boss was plainly amused.

'Oh yes, Mr Randall, absolutely spiffing,' said Verity sweetly and rang off with his laughter in her ears.

She sent out for her sandwich and ate it while catching up on what she would have been doing all morning if she hadn't been playing governess to the landed gentry. She grinned at the thought and forgot about Ben Dysart as she immersed herself in routine. As thunder rolled overhead she made a face, wishing she'd driven into work instead of walking, but her habit was to leave the car at home when she was due in the office all day, as she enjoyed the exercise. It promised to be a wet walk home if the weather failed to clear.

At two o'clock promptly Ben Dysart reappeared, and this time they both avoided personalities by tacit consent, keeping strictly to the workings of Lockhart & Welch. Even so, despite regular interruptions on the phone, the afternoon dragged by interminably, Verity almost disintegrating with relief when it was eventually time to leave. Ben Dysart was highly intelligent and very quick to absorb all the information given him, which should have made her unwelcome task easy, but Verity felt utterly exhausted as she tidied her desk, feeling as though two days' work had been crammed into one.

'Tomorrow, Mr Dysart, I'm due out at two different properties being put up for sale. I imagine Mr Randall considers it a good idea for you to accompany me,' she said briskly.

'He told me to stay close by your side the entire

week,' he said, smiling faintly, 'which from my point of view seems like a very attractive prospect.'

Verity brushed the pleasantry aside brusquely. 'I'll bring my car tomorrow——'

'Haven't you any transport tonight?' he asked swiftly, and cast an eye heavenwards. 'It's throwing it down, Miss Marsh. Please allow me to drive you home.'

'A rash offer—I might live in Birmingham,' she said ungraciously.

'I happen to know you live in Tiddington,' he said surprisingly, and held the door open for her.

'How do you know that?' She looked up at him curiously as she passed him.

'I asked Gussie on Saturday.'

Verity was silenced as they made for his car, parked in the employees' carpark which had once been a stableyard at the back of the building. The small car, its hood up against the weather, proved to be a Morgan, by no means new, but obviously treasured by its owner, who installed Verity inside then inserted his not inconsiderable dimensions behind the steering wheel.

'I saw you in this on Saturday,' remarked Verity as they set off.

'Oh?' He cast a wary look at her.

'You were sprinting down through Gussie's garden, then you stormed past me on your way to the car. I was parked in the layby.'

His profile was unreadable as Verity studied it with faint malice.

'I feel Saturday is one of those days better wiped off the slate,' he said. 'I obviously made a very bad impression.'

'It's really not all that important, Mr Dysart.' Verity gazed through the window through the streaming rain. 'As I said before, it's none of my business.'

'But you disapprove.'

'Nothing to do with me. Except that I feel sorry for Peter.' To her surprise Verity saw this had struck home. A full flush rose in the dark lean cheeks and Ben

Dysart's mouth tightened, his eyes hooded as he concentrated on the road.

'Where exactly do you live, Miss Marsh?'

'Turn right here and it's half way along. The house is called Marshbanks.'

He stopped the car at her gate and turned to her, a hand on her wrist as she prepared to get out. Verity looked down at the hard brown fingers, then up at his hard face, but there was no loosening of his grip.

'You obviously believe the worst of me, Miss Marsh,' he said quietly.

Verity shrugged indifferently. 'As I've said before, I can't see what significance you can possibly attach to any opinion of mine. What you and Gussie get up to behind her husband's back is nothing to do with me. Now I must go—thank you for the lift——'

'Wait, please.' His fingers tightened on her wrist. 'Would it surprise you to learn that I left Tern Cottage only a few minutes after you did on Saturday, and that I haven't been back since?'

'Yes,' said Verity shortly. 'It would.' She shook off his detaining hand. 'Goodbye, Mr Dysart.' Removing herself from the car with more speed than grace, she went up the garden path without looking back, aware that the Morgan stayed where it was until she was inside the house.

The following morning was clear and sunny. Verity woke early with the feeling that something unpleasant was hanging over her, groaning when she remembered Ben Dysart. The day would at least be spent away from the office, and with this thought in mind she got up extra early with the idea of putting in an hour's work at her desk to clear up any backlog of work from the day before.

Verity had two separate wardrobes, the clothes she wore to work and those she wore socially, with a third category—her 'scruff' as Hett called it—kept for housework and gardening. For the trip into the country she chose a casual safari-style suit in beige cotton, tabbed and pocketed, worn with a sleeveless brown T-shirt underneath it, and brown leather sandals with high, but fairly sturdy heels. She brushed her hair ruthlessly and tied it with a brown chiffon scarf, then let herself out quietly to open the garage doors and back out her Mini.

It promised to be a beautiful day, and as she drove through streets relatively empty of traffic at that hour she looked around her with appreciation, enjoying the charm of the town normally so packed with people. Only the night watchman was at the offices when she arrived, though he greeted her without surprise, as it was Verity's habit to utilise this quiet early morning period to catch up on herself when the work piled up during the busy season.

Verity felt a glow of satisfaction at her achievements by the time the usual busy day was in full swing. Summoned to John Randall's office soon after nine she went along to see him with some reluctance, wondering if he had any more unpleasant little surprises up his sleeve.

'Good morning, Verity.' John looked up, smiling. 'Sit down—want some coffee?'

She smiled back warily and accepted his offer, suddenly hungry at the mention of coffee. 'Thank you. I'd love some.'

He picked up the telephone and ordered coffee and a couple of sticky buns, then sat back, his eyes questioning.

'How did you get on yesterday with Ben?'

She shrugged, her face shuttered. 'All right, I suppose. Perhaps you ought to ask him.'

'I did. Last night.' The sleepy blue gaze missed nothing. 'He says you were very helpful, very informative. But at lunchtime yesterday I rather got the idea you were less than pleased. Don't you like him?'

Verity remained wooden. 'You asked me to pass on anything I know about land management and surveying,

Mr Randall. You didn't say I had to like him as well.'

He grinned. 'As bad as that? Funny. From what I hear he usually has the reverse effect on your sex.'

'Possibly——' Verity broke off as Nicola appeared with a tray of coffee and two luscious-looking Danish pastries. 'Lovely—shall I pour?' She smiled warmly at the girl, then handed John Randall a cup of coffee and a pastry, raising an ironic eyebrow at him. 'This is the second time in two days I've been honoured with coffee on a tray. Aren't you afraid I might get ideas above my station?'

He shook his head, munching with enjoyment on his pastry. 'As I've known you since you were a fat little girl in pigtails, I'm not over worried on that score.'

Verity licked her fingers. 'Pigtails yes. Fat, definitely not!' She looked at him very directly. 'Seriously, though, John, if I do get out of hand just cut me down to size. I shan't mind. I'll always be grateful that you took me on.'

John Randall returned her look with interest. 'Your father taught me everything I know about the business when I first came here to work under him, Verity. He would never have employed anyone not worth their salt, and neither would I. I took you on because I thought you were efficient and talented and likely to do a good job for the firm—a chip off the old block, in fact. Which does *not* mean I'm about to give you a rise,' he added. 'Though it has neatly sidetracked the issue of Ben Dysart, or to give him his late description, Capt. B. Dysart, RM—Mentioned in Despatches by the way.'

Verity made a face, impressed despite herself. 'My goodness. A hero to boot. Where did he earn his laurels?'

'Falklands—not that he'd thank me for telling you. Why don't you like him, Verity?'

She avoided his eyes. 'I wouldn't say I don't like him, precisely. We rather got off on the wrong foot, that's all.'

'Do you want me to put him with someone else—I don't know quite who at the moment, now that school holidays have started, but I dare say I can manage something if I put my mind to it.'

Verity shook her head, getting to her feet. 'No, of course not. We're going out today, in any case—the big place outside Chipping Camden and the cottage near Ilmington. He's rather large to be penned up with in my office all day; we'll probably get on better at opposite ends of a tape!' She smiled mischievously. 'Best place for all you chaps, Mr Randall—at arm's length, if not farther!'

'You'll change your mind one day,' he said teasingly.

'Don't hold your breath!' Verity was still smiling to herself when she got back to her office, the smile dying a sudden death at the sight of Ben Dysart, peacefully doing *The Telegraph* crossword. He rose to his feet at once, smiling politely.

'Good morning, Miss Marsh; a much pleasanter day today.'

'Good morning, Captain. It's really quite beautiful, isn't it?' Verity sat in the chair behind her desk, waving him to the other one.

'Not "Captain" any longer, Miss Marsh,' he said quietly.

'Very well, Mr Dysart—perhaps you'd like to know something of the places we intend visiting today. . . .' Verity filled him in on procedures and gave him what information she knew about the vendors, then suggested they get on their way.

'It all looks remarkably tidy in here this morning,' he remarked. 'What happened to that mountain of paperwork?'

'I came in early to clear some of it before we went out.' Verity opened the door, but he gently removed her hand and closed the door again. He stood looking at her in silence. He was wearing a lightweight grey suit with a white shirt and a sober dark blue tie, none of which managed to detract from a certain slight aura of menace Benedict Dysart seemed to wear like a cloak.

'I assume I'm the cause of the extra work?' he asked.

'I often come in early in the summer when we're at our busiest,' Verity answered casually. 'Then I can go out with a clear conscience.'

'Your conscience can surely never be anything *but* clear.' His habit of speaking quietly, almost in a monotone, made it hard to tell whether he was being sarcastic or not. Verity gave him the benefit of the doubt.

'We shall be late, Mr——'

'Couldn't you bring yourself to say "Ben"?' he said swiftly. 'If we're to spend the next few days in each other's company it seems silly to stand on so much ceremony.'

Verity had no intention of becoming even the least bit less formal with Gussie's lover. It seemed to smack of approbation to be on first name terms, yet churlish to refuse, so she gave him what her mother called "Verity's Sunday smile".

'Of course. Shall we go?'

There was a further moment of unpleasantness in the car park, when Verity took it for granted she would drive the Mini, and Ben insisted they travel in the Morgan. He won, Verity refusing to indulge in an outright squabble, and the first part of the drive was accomplished in complete silence.

'A rare gift,' he observed after a while.

'Oh?' said Verity indifferently.

'Silence,' he said. 'Not something the women I know practice with any degree of success.'

This was the wrong remark to make if his intention had been to thaw the atmosphere, as Verity immediately thought of Gussie and retreated even farther into her shell. She spoke only to give last-minute instructions on how to reach their destination, a converted farmhouse rather a long way from anywhere. Ben negotiated the car up a bumpy track and came to a halt in what had once been the farmyard in front of a lovingly restored seventeenth-century farmhouse in the celebrated limestone of the Cotswolds.

Verity jumped out of the car to meet the elderly couple emerging to greet them, introducing Ben to them as 'my colleague, Mr Dysart'. The owner, a tall, white-haired man in his early seventies, screwed up his eyes as he looked at the younger man.

'Dysart? You from Priorsford, young man? Hugh Dysart's boy?'

Ben nodded, smiling, his face lighting up in a way Verity hadn't seen before, and for the first time she began to realise just how potent his attraction could be as he put himself out to be charming to the couple, who insisted on a glass of sherry before Verity and Ben got down to the real business of the morning. By the time the necessary inspection had eventually been made, all the relevant details noted and several photographs taken of the picturesque property, it was lunchtime.

As he drove carefully back down the track Ben asked, 'Where would you like to eat? I know a couple of good places in Chipping Camden.'

'My expenses don't run to that sort of thing,' answered Verity. 'There's a good pub along here—the Lamb & Flag. We can have a ploughman's and a lager.'

A black look passed over the swarthy features for an instant before Ben said stiffly, 'I meant I would stand you lunch, of course.'

'Yes, I know you did, but I'd prefer the Lamb & Flag, if you don't mind.'

Despite his pokerfaced expression it was quite obvious that Ben Dysart did mind rather a lot, the extra-careful way he brought the car to a halt in front of Verity's chosen hostelry only underlining the restraint he was imposing on himself. Without a word he ushered Verity into the room marked 'Lounge', though she would have preferred the saloon bar where a noisy game of darts was in progress. With formality her escort installed Verity on a settle by an open window, and without consulting her went off to get the drinks. Verity sat quietly in the deserted room looking out on a pretty garden where several people were seated at rustic tables, wishing she could join them. Almost before she'd missed him Ben was back with a tray on which reposed a pint of bitter, a pint of lager, and two plates with thick slices of cottage loaf, pats of butter, slabs of cheese and some rather fierce-looking pickled onions.

Verity accepted her portion with private misgivings, never having drunk a pint of lager before, but determined to swallow it all if it killed her. Both hunger and thirst lessened considerably as Ben sat beside her on the settle, the fresh bread sticking in her throat, and the cheese so strong it burnt her tongue. The pickles she left severely alone and after a few minutes gave up all pretence of eating and concentrated on the lager. Ben Dysart seemed indifferent to the silence, and despatched his bread and cheese with speed, though Verity couldn't help noticing he also refrained from the pickles. He drained the last of his pint and stood up.

'Will you have another?' he asked.

Verity shook her head. 'No thanks, I'm fine with this.'

Ben collected the plates and took them over to the bar, returning shortly afterwards with a half pint glass of bitter. As he sat down beside her bursts of laughter came from the taproom from the dart players, and snatches of conversation floated in from the garden, but in the lounge bar all was quiet. For once Verity wished it were the sort of pub that had speakers murmuring forth 'wallpaper' music, because for the life of her she couldn't seem to start up a conversation.

'Are you always such a restful companion?' asked Ben suddenly.

Verity blinked. 'Restful? Don't you mean boring?'

'If I'd meant boring I'd have said so.'

'I couldn't think of anything to say,' said Verity with truth. 'If you want to talk by all means do so.'

'Thank you. Would you mind if I took off my jacket?'

She shook her head and Ben got up, shrugging off the grey suit jacket and putting it over a chair, then he sat down opposite her on a stool instead of resuming his seat beside her. He looked at her with searching black eyes that held hers steadily. 'I have a story to tell. Will you listen?'

Verity stiffened immediately. 'Please, Mr Dysart——' she was saved from saying more as several people came into the room, and their privacy was gone.

Ben stood up, holding out his hand. 'Shall we get out of here?'

Verity consented with such relief there was a wry twist to Ben's wide mouth as he slung his jacket over his shoulder and followed her out of the pub, forestalling her as she would have made for the car.

'What time are you due at the next place?'

'Three.'

Ben looked at his watch. 'It's not two yet.' He gave a quick glance round him, then pointed out a sign further along the road. 'There's a public footpath over there. Will you come for a walk? Please?'

Verity hesitated, then nodded. Ben stowed his jacket and tie in the Morgan, then strolled with her across the road and down the path marked by the sign. It was narrow, between hedges, and for some distance they could only walk in single file, then the path forked, one way leading down to a stream, the other along the edge of a ploughed field. By mutual consent they made for the stream. It was very hot in the sunlight. The heavy rain of the day before had done little to lower the temperature, and when they found a shady tree a little way along the bank Verity was glad to stop and sit on one of the exposed roots, taking off her jacket, and untying the scarf that restrained her hair. Ben remained standing, leaning back against the trunk of the tree, watching the play of sunlight through the leaves on the girl's tanned skin as she gathered up a handful of pebbles and began pitching them into the gurgling water.

'May I continue now?' he asked.

Verity kept her eyes on the water. 'If you must.'

'How long have you known Gussie?' he began abruptly.

'Since we were in boarding school. We were never very close, but at one time she slept in the bed next to mine, and later on we shared a room.'

'Then possibly you already knew of me before we met so unfortuitously last week?' Ben's voice was wry.

'Oh yes, I'd heard of you.' Verity gave him a mocking look over her shoulder. 'Gussie used to go on at length. She was—well—rather informative.'

Ben came down beside Verity and sat where he could see her face. 'How do you mean, informative?'

Verity bit her lip. 'Look, Mr Dysart, I really don't want to get involved—please, don't say any more. I had enough from Gussie last Saturday. You've no need to add anything, really.'

'I'd like to know more,' he said relentlessly, and something peremptory in the very quietness of his voice demanded an answer.

'Well, I gather that when you were both young it was even then a fairly hectic relationship.' Verity was unable to control the curl of distaste on her mouth. 'You'd been on leave just before Gussie came back to school for the last summer term, and, well, she was fairly explicit about—about——'

'Our precise relationship?'

To Verity's surprise the distaste in Ben's voice matched her own. His strong, brown hands were busy breaking up twigs, the snapping sounds sharp in the quiet. Irrelevantly she noticed both hands were scarred, and on the fourth finger of his left hand he wore a worn gold signet ring. She nodded wordlessly in answer.

'I was under the impression Gussie was going to marry me when she came back from that place in Switzerland. They were going to turn her into the perfect wife. For me, as I understood it.' His voice remained colourless as he went on. 'I was—besotted, I suppose—and she was a very lovely creature at that age. I was old enough to know better, but I lost my head. Perhaps you know all the details.'

Verity looked away. 'I don't remember exactly what she told me. I think she intended marrying you at that stage, but then she went off to Switzerland to finishing school, I went to Reading University and we lost touch. We don't move in the same circles much at home. For some reason she did ask me to her wedding—I can remember feeling surprised to see Peter Middleton's name on the invitation instead of yours.'

Ben gave a short laugh. 'I was a younger son, remember, a mere Lieutenant, and at that time not considered at all eligible. I was quite comfortably off, but that wasn't nearly enough for Gussie. She wanted wealth and luxury, and Middleton was exactly the chap for that. I really wasn't any competition.' His face hardened. 'Now my brother is dead things are different, of course. My eligibility has risen astronomically.'

Verity said thoughtfully, 'Gussie said you'd had a row over divorce—she was in rather a state when I arrived on Saturday.'

Ben flung his handful of twigs into the stream. 'Yes. I imagine she was.' He turned to her. 'Perhaps I should elucidate. When I said I was besotted over Gussie, that was a long time ago. I've been all over the world and done a lot of things since then, even fought a war. The callow youth who made a fool of himself over an immature girl no longer exists. I grant you Gussie is still physically as tempting as ever; more so even, now that she's older. It's a pity her intellect hasn't matured to match her body.'

Verity's brows drew together thoughtfully. This man's point of view seemed completely at odds with Gussie's outpourings.

'Why are you frowning?' asked Ben.

She hesitated. 'As you more or less insisted on telling me all this, am I allowed to ask one question?'

'As many as you like.' The sudden gleam of his smile put her back on her guard.

'Why did you go to see Gussie last Saturday—the first time, I mean?' Verity gave him an ironic smile. 'I'm fairly clear about your reasons for the second visit.'

'She invited me to a pre-lunch drinks party—a few old friends, Peter would be *so* pleased to see me again, and so on.'

'When did she ask you?'

'Saturday morning. Gussie said it was an impromptu party, spur of the moment sort of thing. There seemed no particular reason to refuse, so I went. And, of course, there was Gussie all alone; no party. My instinct was to turn tail and bolt, but like a fool I gave in to her persuasions—and stayed.' Ben laughed with grim self-derision. 'After a couple of drinks Gussie, well, she started coming on a bit strong. She asked me to stay the night, as Peter was away. Her idea was that I should creep back after dark, like a criminal. She finally put the wind up me when she started babbling about how she would get a divorce and we could get married. I was in the process of explaining that a few kisses for auld lang syne were one thing, but the offer of the rest was no longer open, when the clock struck three and she threw me out because she was expecting a girlfriend.'

'Oh, bad luck,' murmured Verity with mock sympathy. 'You came down the drive like a bat out of hell—I almost expected you to vanish in a puff of smoke.'

'I was—somewhat aerated,' he said dryly.

Verity regarded him with narrowed eyes. 'Why did you go back?'

Ben met her look head on, his mouth twisting with distaste.

'The landlord of the Bell, Stan Mayhew, is an old pal of mine. I stopped to have a drink with him, being in no mood to go back to Temple Priors. Instead of restoring my common sense the succession of swift shorts I consumed only made things worse.' He looked away. 'You look so cool and judicious sitting there, like a latter day Portia, you may find man's baser instincts hard to understand, but to be honest I thought, in my drunken idiocy, that I might as well go back to Gussie and avail myself of what had been more than readily offered—husband or no husband.'

'I feel I ought to apologise for getting in the way!' Verity's voice quivered with amusement at the thought of the thwarted lover.

Ben snorted. 'Frankly the mere sight of you acted like a douche of cold water. Sanity and sobriety were restored simultaneously in one fell swoop. I shall always be in your debt!'

'I can truthfully say it was nothing,' said Verity dryly. After a moment's reflection she said slowly, 'Your story doesn't tally with Gussie's, though. Her version is that you were the one wanting her to get a divorce, but she couldn't because Mr Middleton Senior had helped her father financially, and had her promise to stay with Peter as collateral.'

'That's news to me,' he said curtly. 'My version is the truth. Whatever cock and bull story Gussie invented was fiction. Which one of us do you believe?'

Verity thought it over, her eyes on the sunlit ripples of the stream. She rose to her feet after a while, looking candidly at Ben as he followed suit.

'I don't have to believe either of you implicitly,' she said calmly, ignoring the hostile look that settled over his features. 'I always take Gussie with a pinch of salt, of course, from previous experience. You I don't know at all, so I'll reserve judgment.'

Ben made no comment as he followed her along the footpath, both of them making for the car in silence, and there was no further conversation until they were on the road heading for Ilmington.

'Just for the record,' said Ben conversationally, 'my parents would dearly like me to marry and provide an heir. Although a lot of the old taboos don't apply any more, they would be somewhat distressed if the bride I chose was obliged to divorce her husband to be eligible for the post. The idea isn't one that appeals greatly to me, either.'

Verity shook her head, sighing. 'Poor Gussie!'

'Why "poor Gussie"?'

'She genuinely doesn't see why she can't have you both—Peter for security and you for kicks.'

'Thanks.' The look Ben shot at her was appalled. 'I know I behaved like a crass idiot on Saturday. I admit it freely. But in extenuation remember that I was once very fond of Gussie, and she's a very persistent and persuasive lady when she wants something. I hope she now thinks of me as a lost cause. Two-timing a man with his wife has never been a practice of mine.'

Verity said nothing, wishing privately she'd never met Gussie Middleton *or* Ben Dysart.

'You know, Miss Marsh,' said Ben reflectively after a while. 'I get the impression you're bored.' His jaw tightened as she made no effort to deny it.

'As I seem to have said at least a dozen times, Mr Dysart, none of this is any concern of mine. I don't want to get involved,' she said with a finality which put an end to any further personal exchanges, the remainder of the afternoon being restricted solely to business.

CHAPTER THREE

VERITY found the rest of the week wearing. The heat continued with unusual tenacity for a British summer, and so did the civil, but cool atmosphere between herself and Ben Dysart. She went to the office early each morning to work in peace before the tension of a day spent in his polite but hostile company. He obviously bitterly regretted confiding in her, at the same time as feeling offence at her refusal to believe in his integrity as far as Gussie was concerned. Verity grew more weary as each day passed, and both Henrietta and Jenny grew concerned, not particularly over the shadows beneath her eyes, but over her very unusual lack of appetite.

On the Friday morning Verity arrived in her office late, feeling much more cheerful. Only one day, then Ben Dysart could be passed on to someone else. She would be free. For once he was before her, busy with his crossword. He looked at her in surprise as he sprang to his feet.

'Good morning. You look very bright and breezy this morning—any special reason?'

'No,' lied Verity, her eyes sparkling. 'Just the thought of the weekend, that's all——'

He raised his eyebrows in polite surprise. 'I thought you were working this weekend.'

She coloured slightly, and applied herself to the morning's mail. 'Well yes, but the weekend is different, somehow.'

Ben leaned against the wall, his hands in the pockets of his beige linen slacks, his face darker than ever against his white shirt. 'Would it have anything to do with the fact that you're getting shot of me today?'

Verity refused to meet his eyes. 'Of course not. Now,

shall we get on? Someone's already interested in the property near Chipping Camden, Mr Randall tells me, apparently they want to see it today with a view to running it as a guesthouse.'

Personalities were forgotten as they both became absorbed in routine, neither of them noticing when the door opened an hour or so later. Verity looked up with an absent smile, expecting Sally with their coffee, to find Mrs Augusta Middleton standing in the doorway, her blue eyes round with astonishment at the sight of the two people sitting close together behind the desk. Ben rose to his feet politely, and Verity smiled more brightly, her heart sinking.

'Why hello Gussie. Come in if you can find room.'

Gussie ignored her completely, looking at Ben with smouldering reproach. 'What on earth are *you* doing here Ben?'

'Trying to learn something about land management, Gussie,' he said blandly. 'May I offer you my chair?'

Gussie flashed a look from Ben to Verity, suspicion in every line of her pretty face.

'He's learning from *you*? Isn't there someone more senior in the firm, better-qualified I mean, to teach him?'

'I do what I'm told, Gussie.' Verity bit back her annoyance with an effort. 'My boss said show Mr Dysart the ropes, so that's exactly what I'm doing.'

Gussie lost interest. She turned to Ben accusingly. 'I've rung you up several times. You can't always be out!'

His face was expressionless. 'Now you can see where I've been.'

'Every *day*?' The idea was obviously unpalatable. Gussie looked more suitably attired for the Cote d'Azur than a morning's shopping in Stratford. Her pale pink trousers fitted her curves closely, her pink halter top displaying a startling amount of bare skin. Huge pink-framed sunglasses were pushed up on her expensively tangled gilt hair, and each upper arm was adorned with

a gold slave bracelet to match the gold hoops in her
ears. In her neat, crisp shirt-dress Verity felt like a drab
sparrow in the company of a bird of paradise.

'I have a lot of time to make up,' said Ben gravely,
and pulled out his chair. 'Do sit down, Gussie.'

She shook her head petulantly. 'I can only stay a
minute.' She turned to Verity, her smile suddenly
returning. 'I say, darling, I hear along the grapevine
that the Wentworths are selling their place near the
Golf Club. Any idea what they're asking?'

'About three times the price of Tern Cottage, at least,
Gussie,' said Verity. 'Have you received all the
paperwork on the cottage, by the way?'

'Yes, darling—what super photographs you took.
You make it sound like paradise by your description,
too. Do you think it will sell quickly? Peter's dead keen
on the Wentworth house—he can raise the price I'm
sure, and you know how he is about his golf.'

Verity shot a questioning glance at Ben, who cut in
smoothly, 'I believe you have a purchaser already,
Gussie. I'm sure I'm not letting any professional cats
out of the bag when I say my father will be contacting
Lockhart & Welch today with a formal offer at the
price your husband is asking.'

Gussie looked stunned. '*Your* father? Why on earth
does he want it?'

'The land beyond the river belongs to Temple
Priors—Tern Cottage would round off the estate very
nicely and provide a home for the new manager.'

Verity felt a quiver of amusement at the blank look
on the other girl's face.

'But you said *you* were—you can't mean—Ben! Do
you want Tern Cottage?' Gussie asked incredulously.

'Not particularly.' Ben avoided Verity's eye and
smiled at Gussie. 'But Father thought it a good idea,
and I suppose it's not a bad idea to have a place of my
own. Don't say you refuse to sell it to us.'

'Couldn't if I wanted to, darling. Middleton Père
actually owns it. It's only nominally Peter's.' She smiled

brightly. 'I don't care who buys it as long as I can have the Wentworth house.' She perched on the desk, looking mockingly at Verity. 'Pity *you* couldn't afford Tern Cottage as you're so mad on it, Vee darling.'

'Great pity,' agreed Verity cheerfully. 'Now, lovely though it is to see you I really must press on, Gussie.'

In an instant Gussie slid off the desk and thrust her arm through Ben's, looking up at him with a pleading pout. 'Come and have lunch with me, darling.' She gave an artful little look over her shoulder at Verity. 'Teacher here can spare her pupil for a while, surely?'

'Take him with my blessing,' said Verity with relief, avoiding the simmering look Ben shot at her over the feathery blonde head leaning close to his shoulder.

'Good of you,' he said without inflection.

'Cheerio, have a nice lunch.' Verity waved them off with great good humour as the door closed behind them, her nostrils wrinkling at the traces of Gussie's heavy perfume lingering in the air. It spoiled Verity's concentration and after a while she opened the door again to let in some air and went in search of coffee, deciding to drink it with three of the other surveyors who were congregated in one office. She endured a good-natured bout of chaffing for a few minutes on her role as instructor to the gentry, giving as good as she got, and arrived back in her office still smiling, pleased to have it to herself for a change. Her good humour dissipated somewhat after lunch, when she returned to find a message waiting for her on her desk. Mr Dysart had rung to say he saw no point in returning for the rest of the afternoon, as he felt he had already trespassed sufficiently on Miss Marsh's time, but wished to convey his thanks for her invaluable help all week.

Verity felt oddly put out. So much for Benedict Dysart's story about Gussie belonging to the past. One little flutter of her eyelashes and he'd gone off to lunch with her like a shot, no doubt with a great deal more than lunch in mind to pass the rest of the afternoon. Verity checked her thoughts irritably. Whatever they were doing, Gussie and Ben were absolutely no business of hers. Without trying to analyse the bleak little feeling of disappointment that hung over her, Verity sensibly gave her full attention to her work with the aim of getting home in good time for her evening with Niall.

All week Verity had been too listless to accept any invitations out for a drink or a game of tennis, wanting nothing more than to lie limply in the garden each evening until the light faded. This Saturday she and Niall had an invitation to a party and tonight they were going to watch Henrietta as a serving maid in *Twelfth Night*. Both prospects pleased, and Niall was obviously delighted to find her so animated as they drove home after the show later that night. Niall Gordon was a fair, amiable young man with a thick blond beard, fond of rugby and squash, and very good at his job. Their conversation inevitably turned to the property market when she invited him in for a drink, though Verity was evasive when he tried to pump her about Tern Cottage, for a number of reasons.

'A little bird tells me you've had Ben Dysart in with you learning new tricks now he's left the service.' His fair-complexioned face was teasing as he took his glass from her.

'Yes. Do you know him?'

'Know *of* him, rather. Bit of a glamour boy isn't he?'

Verity frowned at him in surprise as she sat down. 'He doesn't strike me that way. Rather more the strong silent type I would have said—I don't think I'd like to pick a fight with him, somehow.'

Niall laughed. 'Oh, I don't know. You're not precisely the ultra-feminine helpless type, are you?'

'What is it with me that makes everyone think I'm so invincible?' Verity demanded irritably. 'I'm always the one expected to change light bulbs, mend fuses, put plugs on anything electrical—the list is endless. I even have a friend who's amazed I actually know which holes to put the oil and water in my Mini!'

Niall eyed her uneasily. 'O.K. Simmer down. Next

time I see a puddle I'll throw my coat down for you to trample on—is that better?'

Verity grinned and got up to refill his glass. 'Don't mind me, Niall, it's been a hard week, that's all. I'm not cut out for the role of teacher. To be fair I think Ben Dysart's having difficulties in adjusting, too. It must have come as a shock to him when his brother died.'

'Yes,' agreed Niall soberly. 'The whole thing was pretty grim.'

'What happened? I was up with Mother in Birkenhead at the time.'

'There was a fire in the stables in the night. The Dysarts were away, the stablehand was spending an illicit night away with his girlfriend and by the time help arrived Nick had got the horses out, but the fumes had done for him. He was asthmatic, poor chap.'

'Oh Lord!' Verity was horror struck. 'How terrible!'

Niall nodded. 'My father went to the funeral. I gather his parents were shattered, and Ben just stood between them with a frozen face, trying to comfort them both.'

Verity could picture it. 'Poor things,' she said softly, then changed the subject. 'What party are we going to tomorrow night?'

Niall's face cleared. 'Didn't I say? It's a fancy dress affair for charity—in aid of the local children's home. We're all supposed to turn up in Victorian costume at the Conways. You know what Madeleine Conway is for something different. I think I heard something about dancing on the lawn and all that kind of thing.'

Verity looked at him in exasperation. 'I knew it was at the Conways but you forbore to mention anything about fancy dress. Where on earth am I going to find anything Victorian by tomorrow night, you oaf?'

'Ask Hett. She'll find you something,' he said carelessly and finished his beer. 'I must go, Vee, I'm working tomorrow too. Pick you up about nine, O.K?'

Verity saw him to the gate. 'Do you have a costume?' she asked.

'Bloke at the office dug up some antique cricketing

gear—great fun, I'll look like W. G. Grace. Goodnight, love.' He took her in his arms and kissed her soundly, breaking off as a car came down the road and stopped near by. 'That'll be Hett no doubt. See you tomorrow.' Niall got in the car, waving as Henrietta came in at the gate and strolled up the path with Verity, yawning.

'The show went well tonight, Hett,' said Verity as they went in the house. 'Want a drink?'

'No thanks, Vee. I'm out on my feet. It was packed, wasn't it—good chemistry, I thought.' Henrietta examined Verity's face critically. 'You look a lot better tonight.'

'I feel better—finished my week of tutorial today.' Verity smiled happily.

'Oh, the aristocratic Mr Dysart. He's not that bad, surely?' Henrietta's blue eyes were teasing.

'No, not really,' Verity admitted grudgingly, and changed the subject. 'I'm not tremendously pleased with Niall, either. He's known for ages that the party we're invited to tomorrow is fancy dress and only saw fit to inform me tonight.'

'Oh I say, Vee, how typical! Is there a theme?' Henrietta's sympathy was roused.

'Victorian.'

'Oh well, not to worry—I'll sort something out for you.'

'But I'm working until four, Hett!'

Nothing dismayed, Henrietta soon ironed out the problem, taking Verity's measurements quickly. 'Hold still—there. Done.' She scribbled down the vital statistics and smiled serenely. 'I'll get one of the chaps to run me back after the matinee with some borrowed plumes.'

'You're an angel, Hett, but don't put yourself out— I'll call in at the theatre. I know how tired you get on matinee days.' Verity smiled warmly.

'Fine. Now let's go to bed. I won't promise that the costume will be bang on Victorian, but I'll find something. Are your preferences aristocratic, or poor-but-honest?'

Verity grimaced. 'Definitely not aristocratic! I'd prefer something lower down the scale if you can manage it.'

It was still warm when Verity arrived home with her bundle of loot from the theatre. It had been a busy day, but for some reason she felt full of vitality, her recent malaise vanished like magic, and she unpacked the parcel of clothes with anticipation while Jenny made some tea and took two plates of salad out of the refrigerator.

'I got up early today, it was so hot,' Jenny explained. 'So I thought we'd have tea on the lawn. Prawns suit you?'

'Admirably.' Verity smiled gratefully. 'You're spoiling me.'

'I wasn't doing anything so I thought I'd make myself useful. What have you got there?' Jenny peered at the contents of the parcel curiously.

'I just collected this from the theatre.' Verity chuckled as she deciphered the note Henrietta had put in for her. 'I think these are instructions, but Hett's writing is so diabolical I can hardly make it out.'

They examined the little pile of clothes, chuckling at Henrietta's loose interpretation of a Victorian costume. Her scrawl informed Verity that if she was to be authentically in period a corset was necessary. 'Too hot, Vee, so do your best with this lot—the blouse could do with a wash.'

'A wash!' Verity grinned. 'It's a bit late for that—the sun's still hot, though. Put the salad back in the fridge, Jen, I'll just rinse out the white things.'

A few minutes later a frilled mobcap, a draw-string muslin blouse and a frilly white petticoat were waving gently in the evening breeze while the two girls enjoyed their meal. Jenny laughed when she heard how Niall had neglected to mention that Verity was expected to turn up to the party in costume.

'Men!' she said amiably. 'Why on earth do we put up with them?'

'Goodness knows.' Verity poured out tea and sat back, relaxed. 'Working tonight, Jen?'

'Yes. Richard's on call this weekend, so I'm having nights off on Monday and Tuesday. Oh, by the way, Hett is staying with one of the other girls tonight. She forgot to mention it last night.'

'I dare say I'll manage without you both—sorry you have to work though.'

'Frankly I prefer it to cavorting round in costume, like you and Hett!'

Verity was almost in agreement by the time the necessary ironing was done and she was finally arrayed in the costume. She surveyed her reflection doubtfully. There was nothing particularly remarkable about the voluminous dark red skirt, which looped up over the petticoat to show Verity's slim ankles, nor the low-cut blouse, although the latter left a great deal of smooth brown skin exposed. It was Henrietta's masterstroke that made such a transformation. She had included a quantity of long brown ringlets on a band to fasten under the frill of the saucy mobcap and mingle with Verity's own hair. The result changed her appearance quite startlingly, even to her own critical eye, making her look younger, less self-assured, and for a moment she was tempted to strip the entire outfit off and wear an ordinary dress, but the doorbell interrupted her. She went down on bare feet to let Niall in, feeling self-conscious and slightly embarrassed.

'Verity!' He stood staring at her for a moment, then gave a long, low whistle. 'Well, well! Who's a pretty girl then!'

'You don't think I look silly, Niall?' Verity craned to see her back view in the hall mirror. 'I left it up to Henrietta, but to me the result looks more Nell Gwyn than Victoria.'

He leered at her and stroked his moustache. 'Who

cares? You look terrific—but you don't intend going barefoot I presume?'

Verity frowned. 'No. Help yourself to a drink while I go and rummage.'

A hasty search turned up a pair of soft-soled black pumps once worn to a keepfit class, and with one last look in the mirror Verity went down to Niall, who looked cool in striped blazer and flannels, though more reminiscent of the twenties than the previous century. He put down his drink and slid an arm round her waist, to her surprise, bending his face to hers.

'Seeing you dressed like that, it seems a pity we have to go anywhere,' he muttered. 'I'd rather stay here.'

Verity avoided his seeking mouth and pushed him away impatiently. 'If you think I've gone to all this trouble at such short notice, Niall Gordon, just to stay at home you can think again!'

He sighed and picked up his car keys, looking at her ruefully. 'Why are you never in the mood for, well——'

'Dalliance?' she suggested tartly. 'That's the right word for this get-up, I suppose. I thought we were just good friends, Niall. I've never led you to suppose anything else.'

'I know.' He sighed. 'But one can always hope—come on, let's go.'

The party was in full swing then they got to the Conways, music playing in the extensive gardens, which were lit by subdued lamps strung among the trees. They found their host presiding over the barbecue at the back of the house with the help of several friends. He greeted them with enthusiasm, dressed in nineteenth-century butcher's rig, complete with enormous fake mutton-chop whiskers.

'Very appropriate, Harry,' grinned Niall as he handed over their entrance-money for the charity. Almost at once he and Verity were engulfed in a crowd of laughing friends, everyone in some sort of attempt at Victoriana but few of them very accurate, and no one very critical, though Verity came in for a lot of admiration from the men, somewhat to her embarrassment. She was soon separated from Niall, as first one man then another asked her to dance, but whether it was the abundance of wine, or the unfamiliar clothes, or just the sultry heat of the July night, she felt unaccountably on edge. She ate a little of the food Niall brought her, then danced again, laughing as her partner twirled her round in the waltz that had unexpectedly succeeded the disco music of earlier on. When Verity finally came to a halt, laughing and breathless, she became suddenly aware of the man watching her from the shadow of one of the trees and turned away abruptly, her gaiety quenched, aware that her blouse was slipping off her shoulders and untidy strands of hair lay across her forehead, which felt damp and flushed from her exertions.

Ben Dysart was the last man she either expected, or wanted to see. She kept her back turned in his direction, gratefully accepting the glass of wine Niall brought her and drinking thirstily.

'Isn't that your friend Dysart over there?' Niall gave her a sly grin. 'Have you seen the gear he's wearing?'

'No,' said Verity shortly. 'I didn't notice.' Which was the truth. It was the look in his eyes which had caught her attention, even from a distance making her conscious of tumbled hair and revealing blouse, as though she actually were the easy-going wench her costume suggested. She smiled at Niall brightly. 'I'm going indoors to tidy myself up. See you later.'

Once inside the house Verity made for a cloakroom and did some rapid repairs on her face and hair, retying the cord of her blouse with a jerk and wishing it were time to leave. There was no point in hiding away, she knew, so with head up she went out into the big hall, recognising the figure in the open doorway with a sense of resignation. Ben was standing still, just looking at her in silence, his legs slightly apart, his arms folded across his chest, the clothes he wore making every other man's costume seem silly and artificial by comparison.

In spite of the heat he was wearing heavy boots with gaiters and moleskin trousers, a leather waistcoat open over a striped collarless shirt and a dark red handkerchief knotted at his throat. Verity seemed to have lost the power of speech. They just looked at each other in a silence which intensified and grew, emphasised by the background of music and laughter outside. It was both a shock and a relief when Ben's voice finally broke the silence.

'Pretty Polly Perkins, I assume?' He raised a black eyebrow in caustic enquiry then turned sharply as a familiar fluting voice cried,

'Hello, you two. So this is where you disappeared, Ben!'

Gussie stood under the porch light in all the glory of a hired *fin de siècle* gown in sky-blue satin with low cut bodice and skirt draped into a bustle behind, her hair piled in curls on top of her head. It was a fierce comfort to Verity to note that Gussie looked very hot in her tightly corseted splendour, and with uncharacteristic lack of charity she smiled sweetly and said, 'Don't tell me, let me guess—Lady Chatterley, Gussie?' Verity's hazel eyes glittered as they travelled from Gussie to Ben. 'And you, Mr Dysart, are obviously——'

'A common or garden gamekeeper,' he interrupted brusquely. 'Authentic, I assure you.'

Gussie's eyes narrowed as they took in Verity's ringlets and frills. 'Goodness, darling, not your usual style, all that.' She gestured at Verity's décolletage. 'Frightfully daring—I don't know that it suits you.'

'I disagree with you there,' said Ben, his eyes lingering very deliberately on the area of Verity's anatomy under discussion.

Colour high, Verity moved past him, smiling sweetly at the other girl. 'Peter away again, Gussie?'

Gussie, stiffened, offended. 'No. He's over there somewhere talking to the Conways. We were unforgivably late so he's still apologising, poor darling.'

Verity left Gussie and Ben together, her back very

straight as she went over to Peter Middleton, who was
perspiring in full nineties evening dress, complete with
white gloves and monocle, his face flushed as he talked
to his hosts. He turned to greet Verity with pleasure,
and excusing himself from the Conways, drew her aside
to go into a lengthy discussion on the cottage,
informing her confidentially of Sir Hugh Dysart's offer
and asking whether Verity thought the asking price
could have been higher.

She disagreed, reminding him of the lack of garage
facilities, reluctant to talk business at a party, but not
having the heart to cut Peter short.

'I'd accept the offer, Peter,' she advised. 'This is
entirely unofficial and solely my own opinion, of
course, but I'm sure my boss would agree that you're
unlikely to get a better one.'

His boyish, pleasant face cleared, and he nodded. 'If
you really think so, Verity, then that's it. I'll take your
word for it.' His face softened into a tender smile as
Gussie came up and slid a hand through his own. Ben
was nowhere in sight, to Verity's relief. 'Verity thinks
we should accept Sir Hugh's offer, darling.'

Gussie shot a triumphant look at Verity. 'Fantastic!'
She gazed up at her husband with a melting little-girl
look that made Verity cringe. 'And we *will* be able to
have the Wentworth place, won't we, angel?'

Verity was deeply grateful to see Niall beckoning her
to join a noisy group on the other side of the lawn, and
went over to learn that another means of raising money
for the children's home had been proposed. The ladies
were asked to retire indoors and put some article of
clothing, or jewellery, into a basket, then each article
would be auctioned off to the highest bidder among the
men, who would be entitled to claim a kiss from the
owner once the proceedings were completed. As winner
of the National Competition for Auctioneers Niall was
the obvious choice to conduct the bidding, and hastily
provided with a hammer and a wooden box to pound
on, he took charge.

Verity's first impulse had been to throw one of her gold hoop earrings into the basket, but she changed her mind as a great many others went into the haul, and finally undid the small gold safety pin reinforcing the fastening of her petticoat and, unnoticed, hid it at the bottom of the heap of objects.

Niall was splendid as auctioneer, both efficient and humorous, not allowing the proceedings to drag, or the bidding to go on too long. Large sums were not expected, but there was much hilarity as men bid for and won, garters, earrings, handkerchiefs and a variety of other belongings. Peter made himself rather conspicuous by bidding far too persistently for one of Gussie's easily identified pearl-drop earrings, to his wife's ill-concealed chagrin, and Verity laughed and applauded with the rest as each item went under the hammer, aware that Ben Dysart was back in his former place under the tree, watching the proceedings with enjoyment, but making no attempt to join in.

'And now we come to the final item, ladies and gentlemen,' announced Niall. He grinned as he mopped his perspiring forehead, then held up the last tiny object. 'To those of you unable to make out this minuscule, but very functional object, I would recommend it as useful, if not decorative, fashioned of pure gold, of course, and worthy of a good price for this very deserving cause.' He cast an expectant look around his amused audience. 'Now what am I bid for this genuine gold safety-pin. Do I hear——'

'Twenty pounds,' said a quiet voice.

Niall gave a startled glance in the direction of Ben Dysart and automatically went through the motions of asking for more, finally winding up the proceedings with 'Going once, going twice—sold to the gentleman on my left.'

In the immediate uproar that resulted as men tried to find the owners of the various trifles Verity was glad of the confusion as first one, then another, begged her to lay claim to their spoils. She waited, half-dreading, half-anticipating the moment when Ben Dysart finally confronted her with the safety-pin. There was, of course, absolutely no way he could know it was hers. For that matter she could deny ownership even if he did confront her with it, but when she cast a furtive glance towards the tree he'd been propped against for most of the evening he was nowhere to be seen. To her intense irritation Verity felt deflated.

It was almost an hour later when the party finally broke up and Niall drove Verity home. She felt tired and flat, even though in some ways the party had been great fun. Gussie had enjoyed herself hugely, apparently unaffected by Ben's early departure, dancing with most of the men there apart from her husband, who seemed perfectly content just to stand watching her with an indulgently proud smile that both touched and irritated Verity. She longed to urge him to be more positive with Gussie, not let her ride roughshod over him, but knew it was no use.

The road where she lived was dark and deserted when Niall drew up at Verity's gate. She gave him a quick kiss on the cheek, thanking him for taking her to the party, and was out of the car before he could suggest coming in for a nightcap. She felt restless and out of sorts, very definitely not in the mood for the hassle of rejecting the amorous overtures she was certain Niall would make if she asked him in.

'Ring me,' she whispered hurriedly. 'Good night.'

Verity ran lightly up the path in her heel-less, soft-soled slippers before Niall could protest, glad to hear his car move off before she reached the house. She frowned as she saw a light in her sitting-room, positive she had left the house in darkness when she and Niall left for the party. Shrugging, she unlocked the front door and let herself into the dark hall, every drop of blood in her body seeming to drain away with fright as the sitting-room door opened to disclose a broad-shouldered figure silhouetted against the dim light cast by one single lamp behind it.

'Don't scream,' said Ben Dysart casually. 'It's only me.'

Verity sagged, unable to utter a word from shock, let alone scream. She gazed at him wordlessly, breathing hard, and he moved quickly, seizing her arms.

'Don't faint on me, please.'

'Faint!' Verity's shock melted into red-hot fury and her eyes blazed into his as she wrenched herself out of his grasp. 'As I've been told many times, I'm not the fainting type, Mr Dysart, but I *do* have a temper. What exactly are you doing in my house at this time of night—or at any time of night if it comes to that?' She swung away to switch on the hall light and turned to confront him.

Her intruder just stood there quietly, a faint gleam of admiration on his face as he looked at her flushed, affronted face.

'I frightened you. I'm sorry. I expected to hear your footsteps on the path outside so that I could warn you I was here, but you took me by surprise.' His eyes dropped to the thin, flat ballet slippers on her feet. 'You normally wear heels.'

Verity ignored this. 'How did you get in?' she demanded.

'The kitchen door was unlocked. Are you in the habit of leaving it open?'

Verity flushed angrily. 'No. I must have overlooked it in my hurry to leave for the party. It took me far longer to dress than usual.'

Ben's eyes travelled slowly over her, lingering longest where one ringlet had strayed over her shoulder to lie in the hollow of her breasts, just visible above the drawstring that confined her blouse.

'The result was more than worth it,' he said, something in his voice deepening her angry colour.

'We've now established how you got in,' she said coldly, flicking away the offending curl. 'Now perhaps you'd be good enough to tell me why.'

'I would have thought that was obvious,' he said

instantly, with a sudden glint of white teeth. He took the tiny safety-pin from a pocket in his leather waistcoat and held it up. 'I came to return this—and claim my reward.'

They stared at each other in silence. Verity was finding it difficult to hide the agitation she felt, as her breasts rose and fell quickly, cursing herself for her lack of aplomb. It must have something to do with the clothes she was wearing, she thought wildly, perhaps Victorian palpitations went with the costume, or did one only suffer from those if one wore a tight corset? The absurdity of her thoughts, and a sudden picture in her mind of the spectacle they presented revived Verity's sense of humour.

'You look like the villain of the piece about to ravish the village maiden,' she said, smiling at him for the first time.

Ben moved a little nearer. 'In the stories I've read help always arrived in the nick of time—this is where the hero charges through the door with his axe, or whatever.' An answering smile lit the intensity of his eyes, and Verity looked away.

'How do you know the pin is mine, anyway?' she asked lightly.

'I watched your face. You were laughing and relaxed until then, but you stood so still when your Mr Gordon held up the pin it was obvious—to me, at least.' His quiet assurance irritated Verity intensely.

'Wouldn't it have been a little awkward if Niall had come in with me just now?' she asked tartly.

Ben shrugged. 'You'd never have known. At the sound of voices I'd have disappeared like a thief in the night.' He smiled a little at his own melodrama, and moved nearer.

For once in her life Verity was at a complete loss. She had no idea what to do. If it were any other man she would be offering him a drink, or telling him she was tired and it was late. But no other man was likely to be here under the same circumstances. In her indecision she said the first thing that came into her head, taking the bull by the horns.

'Oh very well—I suppose as you paid £20 for the privilege you may as well take your reward and perhaps I can then see you off the premises.' She closed her eyes and held up her face with sacrificial resignation. There was silence in the room as she waited, and after a time she opened her eyes to find him watching her in amusement.

'Thank you just the same, Miss Marsh, but I've never found it necessary to buy a lady's favours. I paid £20 to the charity, not to you.'

Verity could have scratched his eyes out with enjoyment.

'Mr Dysart,' she said haughtily. 'It's late, I've had a busy day and feel too tired for silly games. I can't imagine what kind of impulse led you to force your way in here tonight, but frankly it's common trespass and I'd be obliged if you'd now leave.'

'I felt the need to retaliate,' he answered coolly, leaning casually against the lintel of the sitting-room door as if prepared for a friendly chat.

'Retaliation for what, for heaven's sake!'

'I dislike being disposed of like the proverbial pound of tea.' His eyes gleamed cold in the subdued light. 'I have an irrational dislike of being told to run away and play. I prefer to choose my own playtime—*and* my own playmate.'

Verity moved nearer, smiling with malice. 'Oh, I see! And there was I thinking you'd be only too pleased to have lunch with Gussie, particularly as that was the last I saw of you for the day.'

Ben's mouth tightened. 'Just for the records, Miss Marsh, I saw Gussie politely off the premises, then had a pub lunch with John Randall, after which I spent the rest of the afternoon upstairs in the auction room.'

This took the wind out of Verity's sails for a moment. 'Well now that's all cleared up,' she said briskly, 'I think it's time you left. I humbly apologise for any offence caused yesterday, I've offered a kiss in return for that ridiculous safety pin—and was turned down—so now I think we can say it's honours even and good night.'

With a negligent lunge he moved swiftly and caught her in his arms.

'I think I'll change my mind,' he said softly, staring down into her startled face. 'Perhaps I'll cash in just slightly on my twenty pounds.' Then he kissed her.

The kiss was neither prolonged, nor violent, nor could Verity honestly say the arms that held her were rough or constraining. She remained quiet in his grasp, making no resistance, but Ben seemed to find her impassivity resistance enough and raised his head after only a few moments to look down wryly into the wide hazel eyes fixed on him with such dispassionate detachment.

'It's a terrible put-down to find you weighing me up instead of joining in,' he said wryly. 'Would you mind telling me what you were thinking?'

'No, I don't mind. But I think you will.' Verity's eyes never wavered.

'Try me.'

'It was just that after watching you with Gussie last week I suppose I expected something more exciting,' she said unwisely, a tremor of disquiet running through her as she saw the unholy flicker in Ben's eyes.

'Fighting talk, Verity,' he murmured, his grasp tightening, and bent his head to hers again. This time it was different. His mouth took control, its pressure prising her unwilling lips apart as one iron-hard arm held her still, the other hand sliding her blouse off her shoulders to caress their smooth contours before finding her breasts, his fingers learning their shape and fullness with a surety of touch that brought the blood drumming to her temples as she fought to free the hands he kept trapped between their bodies. In vain she tried to twist her head away, but he was too strong and too expert, and, she realised with misgiving, no longer in such complete control, at least of himself. His breathing was ragged as he released her suddenly and strode to the door, one of his hands tugging at the scarf round his throat as if it were choking him. Verity stared at his back in breathless resentment, her cheeks flaming as she pulled her blouse up to cover herself, but he kept his face averted.

'I apologise,' he said tersely, and left without a backward glance.

Verity sat down abruptly on the stairs, staring with dislike at the frivolous mobcap and ringlets which had come adrift during the struggle, and now lay on the hall carpet. Ben's attentions had caused no damage to the borrowed blouse, thankfully, but she had learned one or two things from the last few minutes, the glaring lesson being that there were times when it paid to keep one's thoughts to oneself. Wearily she went to bed, but passed a very restless night, the few snatches of sleep she was granted full of dreams where she was being chased by some monster through trees that joined in the pursuit.

It was still early when Verity heard faint sounds and assumed Jenny must have come home early from the hospital. It looked like being another hot day, and it seemed sensible to get up and do a few of her household chores early to leave the rest of the day free for sunbathing. Determinedly she put all thoughts of the night before from her mind and dressed in shorts and suntop before going into the kitchen to fill the kettle.

'Verity!'

She turned round in surprise from slicing bread for toast, to see Henrietta in the doorway looking rather diffident.

'Hett! What are you doing here? Jenny said you were staying the night with someone.'

Henrietta nodded guiltily. 'I was, darling, and I meant to leave a note to say I'd changed my mind, but I forgot.'

Verity grinned and motioned the girl to a chair.

'Have some breakfast—I'll make more toast. Didn't you feel like socialising?'

Henrietta wrapped her rather tatty silk kimono tightly round her slender waist and sat down, accepting a cup of tea gratefully.

'No, Vee, I didn't. It was so hot I felt done in after the performance, so I just came home early and fell into bed, but I woke up later when I heard noises. I was half asleep, really, heaven knows why I decided to investigate—sheer stupidity. I mean what use would I have been if it *had* been burglars?' She gulped the rest of her tea, looking embarrassed. 'I crept out on the landing and there you were in the clutches of some bloke straight out of D. H. Lawrence! I lurked about upstairs in an awful state, wondering if you were about to be raped—after all, darling, if you were you might have been quite happy about it, for all I knew! But then I heard your visitor take off in a hurry so I went back to bed. I didn't like to come down in case, well, you didn't feel like company.'

The funny side of it struck Verity all of a heap. She lay back in her chair, tears of laughter running down her face, Henrietta joining in involuntarily, though somewhat puzzled. Eventually Verity calmed down and explained.

'It's just that the other day I was reflecting—with some regret I may add—that in all my twenty-six years no one had ever, well, *smouldered* over me, then last night, when someone did I was quite frightened—a big girl like me! I rather brought it on myself, by saying something idiotic, besides which the poor man had paid £20 for the honour, so I could hardly blame him.' At the look on Henrietta's face Verity went off into whoops again until the other girl threatened her with greivous bodily harm if an explanation wasn't forthcoming immediately. When she heard Ben had walked into the house through the unlocked back door her eyes grew round.

'You mean he'd been there for some time! Well,

that's nice—perhaps we ought to start a security check every night, landlady.'

'I'm sorry,' said Verity remorsefully. 'I'm not usually so careless, but I spent so much time fiddling with the fancy dress I overlooked it.'

'Did you like it?' asked Henrietta eagerly, then gave Verity a mischievous little smile. 'From my one brief look it was a tremendous success, but I was rather more taken by your friend's get-up—did I actually see gaiters?'

'Yes. Very rustic,' said Verity briefly. 'I've been very rude and forgotten to thank you for the clothes, Hett, they were marvellous.'

'No trouble, darling, but don't change the subject. Who was that gorgeous hunk of man?'

'The one who's been under my feet all week in the office. Ben Dysart.'

CHAPTER FOUR

AFTER their disturbed night both girls were glad to laze around in the garden for most of the day. Jenny came home for a few hours' sleep, then departed to lunch with her Richard while the other two did a little desultory gardening and picnicked on the lawn. Henrietta went indoors to wash her hair later in the afternoon while Verity ironed the newly washed borrowed plumes. She felt hot and restless afterwards, her lack of sleep beginning to tell, so she stretched out on a garden lounger in the sun with a book, but the words kept running into each other and finally she gave up. Seconds later Verity was fast asleep. Henrietta tip-toed past on her way out for the evening and decided to leave her undisturbed. Verity lay motionless, her sleep untroubled by dreams as the sun crept lower in the sky, her skin taking on a perceptibly deeper tone from its rays.

She presented a tempting sight to the man who came round the side of the house a little later on. Ben Dysart stood looking at the sleeping girl, retreated, hesitated, then finally went back.

'Miss Marsh,' he said softly.

There was no response. He lowered himself to the grass by her feet and touched her instep gently. Her foot moved slightly and she muttered something, but her eyes stayed closed. Ben smiled and grasped her foot in his hand, shaking it slightly. Verity's eyes opened wide and stared into his. She blinked sleepily and smiled.

'Is there such a phrase as "unfoot me"?' she asked, yawning, then gathered herself together with an effort and sat up, shaking her hair back.

For Ben Dysart it was by no means the first time he had watched a woman wake up, but it was the first time he had seen one so unselfconscious about the process. Verity made no attempt to tidy herself, obviously waiting for him to speak. He said abruptly,

'I've come to apologise for my behaviour last night.'

Verity stared at him owlishly. 'You apologised last night.'

'I didn't mean it last night; today I do. Sincerely.'

Verity pulled her chair to an upright position and waved him to the other one nearby. He thanked her and pulled it round so that he was facing her. The conventional white shirt and grey trousers of today were in direct contrast with the flamboyantly earthy clothes of the night before, but he looked no less attractive thought Verity idly, then realised he was speaking to her.

'I acted on impulse last night,' he said quietly. 'I behaved in a way quite outside my usual way of doing things. I don't like that kind of party, for one thing, but my mother has quite a lot to do with the orphanage and coaxed me into putting in an appearance. She hunted up the clothes in the attic, so that I wouldn't feel conspicuous.'

'You failed there.' Verity grinned at him. 'You looked so authentic you put everyone else in the shade.'

'Wrong,' he stated, returning her smile. 'Your own outfit won hands down.' He looked at her consideringly, head on one side.

'I'm not normally given to ringlets and frills—we were probably both out of character,' said Verity lightly.

'You may be right; I had no intention of bidding at that auction, I assure you,' he said wryly, 'but when that safety-pin appeared I was certain it was yours.'

'You paid a very fancy price for a mere safety-pin!'

'All in a good cause. Am I allowed to keep it?'

They looked at each other for a moment in silence.

'Are you being facetious, Mr Dysart?' she asked.

'Not in the least—and would it be too much of an effort to say my first name?' he asked impatiently.

'No.'

'Then say it!'

'In my own good time.'

Ben laughed indulgently. 'Have it your own way. Will you have dinner with me tonight?'

Verity was floored. 'Well—I don't know—I don't normally——' she heard herself floundering, annoyed.

'You don't usually what? Accept invitations from uncivilised boors who leap on you at the slightest provocation?' he asked with a wry smile.

'But it wasn't without provocation,' she pointed out. 'I should have kept quiet.'

'And I shouldn't have been in your house in the first place,' he added. 'I ran the Griersons home, do you know them? They live about a mile away, towards Alveston, and when I was coming back along the road here I had the bright idea of paying you a visit.'

'At one-thirty in the morning!' Verity shook her head reprovingly.

'I told you I was off my rocker last night, one way and another. I tapped on your front door with no result, then I thought I heard something round the side of the house and went to investigate and found your kitchen door slightly open.'

Verity stared at him in horror. 'Actually open? I've never done that before.'

'If I were you I'd make sure you never do it again,' said Ben dryly, a glint in his eye. 'You don't want any more strange men frightening you to death, I imagine.'

'No indeed,' she said wholeheartedly. 'When you appeared in my sitting-room doorway I nearly expired with fright.'

'Because it was me personally?' he asked with interest.

'No, of course not, I thought it was someone breaking and entering. I'm not the nervous type, but that was a bit much. Silhouetted against the light like that you looked very menacing, I assure you.'

'I'm sorry. I was a crass idiot.' Ben paused, his eyes

very direct as they met hers. 'I don't think I'm entirely to blame for the second transgression, though, Verity. That was a hell of a challenge to throw at a man.'

'I know, I know,' she said hurriedly, her eyes falling. 'I've admitted it already, so we'll forget all about that bit, shall we?'

'Easier said than done. Trying to forget about it gave me a very bad night,' he said with feeling.

Verity shifted uncomfortably in her chair, hoping the sunset was sufficient to account for the heightened colour in her face. Ben sat relaxed, legs crossed, looking at her.

'Well,' he prompted. 'Will you come out for a meal?'

'I don't really think it's a good idea——' she said slowly.

'You mean Gordon might object?' he cut in coldly.

'No, I don't. Niall is not in a position to object.' Verity sighed, deciding there was no point in being evasive. 'It's Gussie I'm thinking of.'

Ben was obviously having difficulty with his habitual self-control.

'In words of one syllable, Verity, now that Gussie's someone else's wife she's no longer any concern of mine except as a friend. The silly incident you witnessed was one isolated happening which will never occur again, believe me. Other men's wives are not my scene, I assure you.' He shook his head in wonder. 'Hell's bells, is it always such hard work to get a date with you? You must have very hardy men-friends.'

'I believe in cards on the table,' said Verity tartly. She shot a penetrating look at his set face. 'Can you deny you still feel something for her?'

'No,' he said reluctantly. 'I was very fond of Gussie when I was young, I'll admit. But it's different now. We're——'

'Just good friends!'

'Do I have to renounce all other women before I merit your company?' he asked with sarcasm, 'or are you satisfied now?'

Verity looked at him levelly. 'You've got the wrong end of the stick. You and Gussie can do what you like as long as I'm not involved.'

'I'm fast coming to the conclusion your company at dinner is just not worth the aggro, Miss Marsh,' Ben said wearily.

'I thought we'd progressed to first names,' she pointed out.

'Funny you should say that. So did I.' He gave her a formal, unsmiling nod. 'Goodbye. No doubt we'll run into each other some time.'

Verity chewed her bottom lip pensively as Ben Dysart strode down the garden, then she shrugged philosophically and went indoors, not really sorry to be staying in. There was nothing restful about the man, and she felt tired after every encounter with him. Niall's company was infinitely less demanding. Nevertheless, when Niall rang up later suggesting they went out for a drink Verity pleaded fatigue and went to bed early, feeling vaguely dissatisfied with life.

Monday was odd. After resenting Ben's presence in her office all the previous week Verity now found she missed it. She was out a great deal during the rest of the week, which helped, and only saw Ben once in passing. He greeted her courteously, a polite stranger again, and went on his way. Verity was relieved, she thought. In the evenings she played tennis and read quite a lot in bed, where she retired early every night. Niall was one of her tennis partners, as was Jim Hayward, a young accountant with a punishing forehand and a zany sense of humour, but Verity found she had no inclination to linger over a drink afterwards, pleading pressure of work and the need for beauty sleep.

Towards the end of the week her Mini refused to start at the end of a very hectic day. After several abortive attempts Verity locked the car in frustration, looking up quickly at a light touch on her shoulder. Ben stood looking at her in polite enquiry.

'Problems?' he asked pleasantly.

Verity nodded ruefully. 'Dead as a doornail.'

He held a hand out for the keys and got in the Mini.
When he turned on the ignition he got the same
response as Verity, a mere lethargic drone or two from
the engine. Ben glanced at the dashboard and raised an
eyebrow.

'Your lights are on. When did you use the car last?'

Verity felt two inches high. Her colour rose. 'When I
came in this morning—I haven't been out since. I
suppose I just didn't notice in this bright sunshine.'

Ben gave her rather a supercilious grin and went over
to the Morgan, but came back with an impatient frown.

'I forgot. Mother borrowed my jump leads yesterday
and still has them. The best thing I can suggest is that I
take your battery home with me and recharge it
overnight. I'll bring it back in the morning——'

'Oh, but I couldn't put you to the trouble,' began
Verity at once, more embarrassed by the minute.

'No trouble,' said Ben shortly, and within minutes
the offending battery was removed from under the
Mini's bonnet and placed in the Morgan.

'I'm most grateful,' said Verity with an effort, very
put out at being obligated to Ben Dysart, of all people.
'I could have had someone come from a garage in the
morning.'

'Pretty pointless when I can do it just as easily—and
for a much smaller fee,' Ben said, poker-faced as usual.

'*Smaller* fee?' Verity wasn't keen on the sound of
that. 'What exactly had you in mind?'

'I thought perhaps we could actually achieve that
meal together—minus all the debate this time,' he
added casually.

Verity smiled politely. 'How can I refuse?'

'Tonight?'

She shook her head. 'No. I'm afraid not. I'm going out.'

'Tomorrow, then,' he said with finality.

'Yes, fine. Tomorrow.' Verity was unprepared for the
peremptory hand on her elbow that propelled her
towards the Morgan.

'I'll run you home.' Something in the way Ben said it made Verity get in without a word. The silence continued all the way home. It hardly augured well for the success of an evening out together, and Verity cursed her own carelessness for leaving her lights on. The strap of her handbag must have caught in the switch, she could think of no other explanation. It was a relief to arrive home, and Verity thanked Ben formally and rather distantly for his help as she got out.

'I'll pick you up at half-seven tomorrow,' he said, and raised a hand in farewell as he drove off.

Niall Gordon had obviously come to the erroneous conclusion that he had sole copyright on Verity's spare time. He looked taken aback, then distinctly annoyed that evening after the cinema when Verity told him she was booked for Friday night.

'Booked? What do you mean?' he demanded indignantly. 'We always go out together at weekends.'

'There's no hard and fast rule about it, Niall.' Verity was by no means pleased at his tone.

He tossed back the remainder of his drink and stood up. 'I was rather under the impression there was. Shall we go?'

They left the wine bar in silence and walked quickly down Sheep Street to the car. Niall opened the door for her frostily and drove off with something less than his usual care.

'Am I allowed to ask who stole a march on me?' he asked with dignity.

'Ben Dysart.'

'Oh I see.' Niall scowled ahead of him like a sulky schoolboy. 'Big guns, Verity—out of my league. No wonder I lost out.'

'Oh for heaven's sake!' Verity lost her patience. 'I'm merely having a meal with the man. I could hardly refuse, he's recharging my car battery.'

'Oh yes,' he sneered. 'I bet that's not all he wants in return, from what I hear.'

Verity had had enough. When Niall stopped the car outside her gate she jumped out at once. 'Good night, Niall. Thank you for taking me to the cinema, but I won't ask you in, you're obviously in no mood to be rational.'

'No, I'm not!' He glared at her through the open window. 'Perhaps we'd better forget Saturday night, too.'

'Perhaps we had.' Verity smiled coldly and shut her garden gate behind her with a decisive click, walking away quickly with head high.

She walked to the office fairly early next morning and had been at her desk an hour or so when Ben Dysart tapped on her door.

'Good morning. If you'll let me have your keys I'll start your car up once I've put the battery back—it's fully charged now.' He held out his hand.

Verity took the keys from her bag and handed them over.

'I could easily do that myself,' she pointed out.

'No doubt. But I'm more easily spared than you are.' He smiled briefly. 'I'll report in a few minutes.'

In Ben's absence Verity asked one of the juniors for two coffees, and was able to offer a freshly-made cup to him when he returned. Ben looked surprised, but thanked her, sitting on a corner of her desk to drink it. He tossed the car keys to her.

'Your Mini started up first time,' he said. 'Why were you driving with lights in this weather?'

'I wasn't. Something must have caught in the switch, and I wouldn't have seen they were on in this sunshine.' She smiled politely. 'It's wonderful weather, isn't it? I keep feeling it must break.'

'Progress indeed,' he remarked with a chuckle. 'If we can actually discuss the weather things are looking up!'

'Perhaps we ought to make a new start,' said Verity impulsively, then bit her lip, frowning, wondering if her words were misleading.

Ben's hard features held a look of amusement as he

stood up. 'Don't stop to think twice about everything you say, Verity. Your candour is one of your greatest charms.'

Verity fluttered her eyelashes coyly. 'Compliments, Mr Dysart? You're spoiling me!'

He grinned and opened the door. 'See you tonight— be ready.'

Verity shook her head in amusement and got on with business of the day.

With no idea where Ben was likely to take her Verity was undecided what to wear. She arrived home in good time for a leisurely bath, and a chat with Jenny while she was getting ready.

'The faithful Niall, I presume?' Jenny was lolling on Verity's bed watching her do her face.

'No, not tonight. I'm having dinner with Ben Dysart,' said Verity casually, her attention on the mascara wand she was flicking at her eyelashes.

Jenny raised her eyebrows. 'Your gamekeeper? It should be a more interesting evening than the usual thing with Niall, anyway.'

Verity turned in surprise. 'Don't you like Niall, Jen?'

The other girl shrugged. 'He's all right. I have a nasty suspicious mind, that's all.'

'You mean he's got a few of us on the go simultaneously?'

'Not him! Too expensive.' Jenny smiled scornfully. 'No. I just think Niall's on to a good thing, that's all. A girl with a very good job, a car and a house of her own in a very desirable part of Stratford—what more could an ambitious young man want?'

Verity turned away thoughtfully. 'You think my possessions are the main attraction then?' she said slowly.

Jenny was instantly remorseful. 'No, of course not, Vee. But they're no disadvantage either. If you're dithering about what to wear,' she added, 'my vote goes to that one.' She pointed to one of the three dresses hanging outside Verity's wardrobe.

From the look on Ben Dysart's face, when he appeared on the stroke of seven-thirty, Jenny had been right. The dress was knitted in cobweb fine yarn in edible shades of honey and cream and chocolate, sleeveless and V-necked, with a slim skirt that fluted a little towards the hem. Simple and understated as a sweater, the dress had cost Verity a pretty price, but was worth every penny as a standby for special occasions. Unaware until that moment that she considered this evening as special Verity gave a friendly smile of welcome to Ben, who was dressed in his habitually conservative fashion, in fawn trousers and cream shirt, with a fawn cashmere sweater knotted round his shoulders by the sleeves.

'You look very attractive, Miss Marsh.' He returned her smile and glanced at his watch. 'Punctual too.'

'I hardly dared be anything else—I was Verity this morning,' she added.

'And shall be tonight then. I thought it best not to be too familiar,' he said with a straight face. 'I'm straining every sinew in an effort to remain in your good graces.'

Verity laughed, suddenly very much at ease as they drove off. The constraint that always seemed to lie in wait when they were together was missing this evening, and they talked without effort on a diversity of subjects while they ate a very good meal in a country pub not far from Broadway, Ben obviously well known to the landlord and all the staff. Verity refused offers of steak au poivre and chicken Marengo in favour of a selection from the cold buffet, thoroughly enjoying succulent rare roast beef and game pie, accompanied by an imaginative salad. Ben chose the same dishes, augmenting his plate with home-baked ham and a slice of turkey, but refusing the syllabub that Verity found impossible to resist for pudding.

'I like to see a woman eat properly,' he said lazily, as they lingered over coffee and brandy.

Verity twirled the Remy Martin in her bubble-shaped glass, her lips twitching.

'When my appetite showed signs of flagging my mother hauled me off to our doctor immediately, which gives you a general idea of my eating habits. I have to be in pretty dire straits to go off food.'

'An engine needs fuel to keep running, and you drive yourself pretty hard.' Ben leaned back in his chair, smiling. 'Not that it seems to affect the trimness of the chassis, to continue the theme.'

Verity grinned. 'I'm tall. The calories have a fair distance to cover before they make very much impression.'

He stood up and held out his hand. 'Let's go back to our window seat in the other room.'

'Someone's sitting there,' said Verity, as they dodged their way through the crowded room, but to her surprise the young couple rose at their approach and surrendered their seats, the boy giving Ben a conspiratorial wink as he passed.

'Son of the landlord.' Ben looked smug at the look of surprise on Verity's face. 'I paid for a couple of drinks for young Sam and the girlfriend and he kept our seats warm.'

He looked very pleased with himself, his face so much younger when it was relaxed. Verity asked curiously, 'How old are you, Ben?'

'Thirty-two—how old are you?'

'Twenty-six,' she answered absently, secretly surprised. She had thought him much older.

'You obviously thought I was *forty*-two,' he bantered.

'No. But I did guess a bit more than you said,' said Verity honestly.

'We men don't resort to artifice to disguise the march of time,' he said quizzically. 'A man has to accept age as it comes, warts and all.'

'Oh I don't know—one only has to watch television to see make-up and hairdye in abundance on members of your sex, Mr Dysart!'

'For God's sake stick to Ben!'

'I was only joking,' said Verity gently.

'Yes, of course. Sorry. What may I offer you to drink?'

Verity shook her head regretfully. 'After Martinis, wine *and* brandy, I think I'd be pushing my luck if I had anything else.' She looked at him reprovingly. 'You drank far less than me.'

'Not much option, ma'am, I'm driving.'

'Next time I'll drive——' Verity stopped short, colouring painfully at the careless assumption in her words.

Ben leaned across and touched her hand fleetingly. 'Thank you. When do you suggest "next time" should be?'

Verity smiled at him ruefully. 'What good manners you have. You're not obliged to take me out again just because I spoke without thinking.'

'I'm not taking you out—you're taking me!' He laughed, a sudden cajoling look in his black eyes. 'I suppose it would be asking too much to wonder if you're free tomorrow night?'

Verity gave a crooked little smile. 'No. As it happens you wouldn't.'

Ben gave her a sharp look, his black brows drawn together. 'Young Mr Gordon away?'

She shook her head. 'I don't think so.'

'A rift in the lute? Genuine interest, I might add, not idle curiosity,' he added quietly.

'I suppose you could put it like that. To be more precise I think we rather got our lines crossed about the exact nature of our relationship. On my part it was just friendship—on Niall's, well, he seemed to consider it a lead up to something more. A lack of communication somewhere—probably entirely my fault.'

'One can hardly blame him, Verity,' Ben said reasonably. 'You're physically attractive, good at your job, you have a home of your own, I gather——'

'Who told you that?'

He made a face at her. 'I hate to bring up her name,

but it was Gussie. I would hardly have had the effrontery to walk into your house last night if you'd had an angry father and a couple of large brothers!'

Verity gave him a look of prim disapproval. 'But you had no conscience about terrifying a poor defenceless female?'

Ben had the grace to look a little uncomfortable. 'Put like that it *does* sound a bit grim, but in extenuation all I can say is that I acted on the spur of the moment when I found the house empty and a door conveniently open. I humbly apologise once more, Verity.'

He was obviously taken aback by the smile of mischief she turned on him.

'Actually, the house wasn't empty!' she informed him.

Ben looked thunderstruck, dark colour rising along his cheekbones.

'You had someone staying with you?'

'I always do. Gussie forbore to mention that I have paying guests!'

'Good God! Did we—did I, I mean did they hear——?'

'Yes,' said Verity unkindly, enjoying his flounderings hugely. 'Both my paying guests are female, by the way; Jenny's a nurse and she was working that night, but Henrietta's an aspiring young actress with the RSC, and we woke her with our little clash. She crept out on the landing, quivering with fright, to see you and me in, well——'

'Impassioned embrace,' Ben said matter of factly.

'As you say.' Verity's lips twitched. 'She was undecided whether you were breaking and entering, but I think your costume rather scotched that. Then she was worried that you had rape in mind, but in that case thought I might be annoyed if she interfered—so she went back to bed.'

Ben's sudden crack of laughter broke through even the hubbub of the busy lounge bar on a Friday night.

Several faces turned in amusement, and he quietened down immediately.

'She had no idea of coming to your aid, then,' he said, chuckling.

'Henrietta weighs about seven stone and looks as though a puff of wind could blow her away, so I think she did the sensible thing.' Verity's eyes danced. 'I'm a big strong girl, after all.'

Ben shook his head. 'Not all that much, Verity. If your friend's suspicions had been correct there would have been little you could have done to prevent me—or any other male with rape on his mind.'

Verity realised Ben was deadly serious and thought that one over. 'It's a good thing your intentions were quite different, then.'

'I don't think my intentions would have borne scrutiny for a few moments there last night, but luckily common sense took over before I made a complete fool of myself.' His eyes held hers intently, and Verity flushed.

'I think we should forget all about it,' she said lightly, glad when he rose to his feet.

'If we're not going to drink anything else perhaps we should give way to someone who is,' he suggested. 'Shall we go?'

They talked on less emotive subjects on the way home, Verity wondering if she should ask Ben in when they arrived. Ben left the car idling when they drew up outside, obviously not expecting to be invited in, so Verity thanked him with sincerity for a very enjoyable evening and prepared to get out.

'Hang on. You haven't said where you intend taking me tomorrow night,' he reminded her.

'Do I have to take you somewhere? I'll give you a meal here if you like.' Even as the words left her mouth Verity regretted the impulse, but it was too late. Ben was obviously very pleased.

'I'd like that very much. Thank you. Good night, Verity.'

'Good night,' she said faintly, her words lost in the sound of the engine as he put the car in gear and drove away.

CHAPTER FIVE

VERITY fully expected to lie awake all night, worrying about the deeply regretted dinner invitation, but she slept like a log all night, surprised when she opened her curtains on grey drizzle the following morning. The heat-wave had petered out into rain instead of the expected storm. With no temptation to lie in the garden Verity did her tidying up early, making as little noise as possible to avoid disturbing Jenny, her mind busy with thoughts of what to give Ben to eat. It was only when she was making her bed that she realised she had a problem not only of what to feed her guest, but where. The one-time dining room was now her bedroom, and the kitchen was very much a kitchen, with no dining area as in more modern houses. The garden would have been the answer if the weather had held up, but as it was Ben Dysart would just have to picnic in the sitting-room and like it.

She was still abstracted as she drank a mid-morning coffee, looking up with an absent smile as Henrietta came in and sat down at the table sleepily.

'Can I scrounge a cup, darling? I've run out—must do some shopping this morning.'

Verity obliged, Henrietta watching her closely.

'Something the matter, Vee?'

Verity nodded, sighing. 'I've invited Ben Dysart here for dinner tonight.'

'Here? Crumbs, love, what came over you?'

'Good question. Must have had too much to drink.'

'He wined and dined you right royally, then?'

Verity brightened. 'He did. A pub somewhere near Broadway. We had a very good meal. In fact I enjoyed the evening much more than I expected.'

'Did you now! Niall's nose will be put out of joint

good and proper.' Henrietta smiled knowingly. 'How come you're not seeing *him* tonight?'

'We had a slight difference of opinion,' said Verity, and changed the subject. 'Come on, if you want to go into town I'll give you a lift. Got any suggestions about my menu for tonight?'

Verity was a fair to middling cook, with two or three recipes kept for special occasions, all of them provided by Henrietta who advised her to stick to one she already knew. A Basque recipe was decided on, chicken breasts cooked with onions, tomatoes, peppers and garlic, and Verity bought cheese to follow it, with the idea of keeping things simple. The money that would have been spent on a first course and a fancy pudding was used to purchase a good wine, and Verity and Henrietta went home to eat a sandwich lunch together before the latter went off to her matinee and Verity put the finishing touches to her housework. As soon as Jenny was up and away to her Richard, Verity ran the vacuum cleaner over her domain, before setting to with Henrietta's version of 'Poulet Basque'.

When Ben Dysart arrived Verity was sitting on the sofa watching a film on television, halfway through a Campari and soda, perfectly cool and collected, with everything in hand. She opened the door to him with a smile which widened as he held out a bottle of wine with one hand and a bunch of perfect apricot-tinted roses with the other.

'Good evening,' he said, smiling. 'A small token of appreciation.'

'Why thank you.' Verity sniffed the roses with delight as she showed Ben into the sitting-room. 'What a heavenly colour.'

'From my mother's garden—Beauté is the official name, her particular passion.' Ben gestured towards the wine. 'Chambréd, Verity, if I may make the suggestion.'

She gave him a mocking little curtsy. 'You may. You may have the privilege of opening it too—this is where we're eating, so I'll leave it here.'

Verity flew to the kitchen for the gin and tonic Ben requested and found a white Coalport bowl of her mother's in one of the cupboards for the roses. She took it back with the drink and proceeded to arrange the flowers unselfconsciously while she was talking to Ben.

'When I thought about it afterwards my offer of a meal wasn't much use as far as your alcohol consumption is concerned, Ben.' She smiled at him apologetically and turned back to the roses. 'You still have to drive yourself home.'

Ben sat relaxed in one of the chintz-covered armchairs, watching her deft, graceful movements as he sipped his drink.

'The success of an evening is not how much, or even what one drinks.' His sudden smile lit his face as she looked up from the completed rose-bowl. 'It's the company in which one drinks it.'

'Prettily said!' Verity returned to her seat on the sofa and picked up her glass in salute. 'I'll drink to that.'

'How do you normally spend Saturday evening?' he asked casually.

She shrugged. 'It depends. A meal out somewhere, like last night, sometimes just drinks, occasionally the cinema or the theatre.'

'And always with Gordon?'

Hazel eyes met black ones levelly. 'Yes, but invariably with a group of other people too—most of us in the same line of business, or something connected. We tend to talk shop rather a lot, which makes us a bit insular, I suppose.'

'And last week you had me on your plate as well.' The corners of Ben's wide mouth went down. 'You must have cursed John Randall when he wished me on to you.'

'Yes,' agreed Verity candidly. 'Especially after——' she stopped abruptly.

'After the inauspicious manner of our first meeting,' he finished for her. Verity nodded, looking at him speculatively for so long his eyebrows rose in query. 'What are you thinking about, Verity?'

'I'm beginning to realise that you laugh at me most of the time behind that poker-face,' she said. 'Why do you wear such a mask?'

He hesitated for a moment. 'I've never told anyone this before, but when I first went away to school the only way I could stop myself howling from sheer homesickness was by keeping my face rigid. I missed my parents like hell. One was not expected to get emotive at school, so I learnt to hide my feelings the best way I could. I got over the homesickness eventually, but the facial habit stuck.' Ben kept his eyes on his drink while he was talking, almost as if he were embarrassed, then he drained his glass, looking up to meet the warm sympathy in Verity's eyes head on. She got up to take his glass.

'Poor little boy. Gussie and I cried our eyes out every night at the beginning, but everyone else did as well, so we soon got over it. Let me get you another drink.'

Ben shook his head. 'I'd rather reserve my palate for whatever smells so inviting in your kitchen.'

'It might be as well to reserve judgment until you've eaten it,' Verity warned gaily. 'I'm not much of a cook.'

Ben's rather touching little confession seemed to add a further measure of warmth to the evening, which flew by on wings. The chicken dish had turned out well, to Verity's relief, enhanced by the full, smooth red wine brought by Ben, and they talked easily while they ate, the informality of eating from plates balanced on their knees making for an intimacy a more formal meal might have lacked. Verity was gratified when Ben polished off a second helping of her casserole, and ate quite a quantity of the Stilton that followed it. She was enjoying herself immensely, and was fairly sure that Ben was too, which made her pang of disappointment all the sharper when he rose to go just before midnight. Outside the rain had stopped and the atmosphere was thick and oppressive as she walked to the gate with him. Ben paused before opening it.

'I've enjoyed this evening very much,' he said, taking her hand. 'More even than last night.'

Verity said nothing, wondering why he felt it necessary to vanish before twelve on each occasion if he meant it.

'Shall I see you next week?' he asked.

'It's highly likely if you're still coming into the office every day,' she said, deliberately obtuse.

Ben raised his other hand and touched her cheek with a hard forefinger. 'You know quite well that wasn't what I meant.'

Verity kept her eyes steadfastly on the glimmer of his white shirtfront and said nothing. He waited, then laughed softly, with an indulgence that relegated her to the nursery. 'May I take you out again on Monday evening, Miss Marsh?' he asked with exaggerated formality.

'Why?' asked Verity baldly.

'Must I have a reason?'

'Yes.'

'I enjoy your company. Isn't that the normal thing?'

'I suppose so.' Verity sounded doubtful. 'But it's slightly different in our case——'

'I fail to see why. Now. Answer me. Monday—yes or no?'

'I suppose so,' she said almost grudgingly.

'Don't overwhelm me with enthusiasm! I'll pick you up at seven-thirty.' Ben squeezed the hand he held and let it go. 'Thank you for a delicious meal. Good night Verity.'

'Good night,' she echoed automatically, and turned on her heel and stalked up the garden path before he had time to start up the Morgan. There is nothing more annoying, she thought, than to feel annoyed without any real basis for the emotion.

During the week that followed Ben not only took her out for a drink on the Monday, but monopolised the rest of the week as well. Verity insisted on leaving Tuesday and Thursday free for a game of tennis, but under the circumstances neither evening proved very happy, as she came in for a lot of stick from Niall, who was so off-hand as to border on rudeness. She was surprised at how much she enjoyed her evenings with Ben. His company was stimulating and he was a good listener, interested in her childhood and background, and sometimes coming out with odd bits of reminiscence about his own. He was inclined to reticence on his military career, unwilling to discuss his Falklands experiences on the one occasion Verity made a tentative overture on the subject from sheer interest, but now and then coming out with one of the more humorous incidents in his service life.

'Do you miss it?' Verity asked. The fine weather had returned, and after a meal at Marlowe's in the town they were stretched out on garden chairs on the lawn, watching the stars pierce the ink-blue dusk one by one.

'Not so much now—I've been out quite a while. My time's taken up with trying to pour myself into a new mould.' Ben sounded resigned, with an underlying note of sadness. Accustomed by now to his undemonstrative face Verity was learning to detect nuances of expression in his voice as guidelines to his feelings. She wondered if the sadness was due to his brother's death, or whether Ben still felt some lingering regrets in his heart for Gussie, despite his denials. Telling herself to stop indulging in sentimental twaddle, she got up and took his glass.

Ben caught her hand. 'No more for me, Verity. Would you sit down again, please? I'd like to talk to you.'

'I thought we were talking.' Verity was glad to sit down as it happened. Some new note in his voice seemed to have affected her knees.

'I was working up to changing the subject,' he said, and was silent for a while before going on. 'Verity, are you involved with anyone? Romantically or sexually, I mean?'

Verity stiffened. 'No,' she admitted reluctantly.

'Have you ever *been* in love with a man?'

'No, I don't think so.'

Ben chuckled softly. 'I think you'd be sure if you had.'

'You, no doubt, are better qualified to judge,' she said acidly.

'Possibly. Let me put it this way. I know we made our acquaintance in just about the worst possible manner—and it took you some time to rid yourself of the opinion that I was a two-timing bastard ready to jump into bed with another man's wife at any convenient opportunity.'

'Circumstantial evidence was rather against you,' said Verity reasonably. 'To be very honest I don't know that I'm entirely sure on that particular issue even now.'

She could hardly see Ben in the gathering darkness, but she knew very well he was angry, his tension communicating itself to her quite plainly.

'Only time will substantiate my assurances, appar ently,' he said with irony. 'For the moment I rest my case. What I was trying to say, however, is that now I think we're on a different footing. I enjoy being with you, and I'm fairly certain you enjoy being with me. You're too honest to spend time with me if it isn't at least moderately agreeable to you. Am I right?'

'I suppose you are,' she said slowly, half afraid of where all this was leading. 'But I know several men whose company comes in the same category.'

'Do any of them want to marry you?' he said swiftly.

'Well, no.' Verity frowned in the darkness. It was galling in the extreme, she found, to be forced to admit it.

'Have you been waiting for the love at first sight of popular romance, Verity? Were you hoping that some day your prince would come?' The sarcasm stung her on the raw.

'I'm not aware that I've been waiting for anything, or any *one*,' she snapped. 'Why should I? I have a job I love, a lot of friends, I already possess a home, not to mention a loving mother and a very nice stepfather ready to welcome me with open arms any time I wish. I've never been conscious of the slightest lack. This romantic love you talk about just isn't my style. I'm fairly sure it would embarrass me if ever it did rear its unlikely head!'

'Exactly!' The satisfaction in his voice was positively smug. 'My reading of your character in a nut-shell. From the start I felt you were more interested in the practicalities of life rather than the world well lost for love.'

Verity had had enough. She got to her feet irritably. 'I'm going in for some coffee,' she said curtly. 'Do you want some, or is it already past your bed-time—I can't see my watch.'

'As I've by no means finished yet,' he said patiently, 'perhaps you won't mind if I have some coffee too. At my age one needs a stimulant to keep awake after eleven.'

The irony in his voice made Verity grin unwillingly as she switched on the lights in the kitchen. He sat on a corner of the kitchen table, looming large in the small room as she poured boiling water into two mugs and handed him one.

'Only instant, I'm afraid. Sugar and milk on the tray.'

Ben looked at her curiously, as if wondering why she seemed annoyed.

'Shall we sit in your drawing-room for a few minutes while I finish my spiel?' he suggested. 'Having gone this far I'll finish if it kills me, or at least before I begin to wonder if it's worth it.'

Verity stalked ahead of him with dignity, switching on the lamps in the homely, comfortable room that had never rejoiced in the title of 'drawing-room' before. She sat down on the sofa with an air of exaggerated patience, stiffening when Ben turned off all the lights except one before sitting beside her.

'Right,' he said, in a businesslike way that

antagonised her even further. 'Let me map out my suggestion. You apparently neither require nor welcome the idea of the so-called *grande passion*. Having experienced it myself I think you're very wise—it's not to be recommended as a way of life, I assure you.' He paused, as if expecting her to say something, but Verity preserved a dignified silence. 'On my part,' Ben went on, 'I like you a great deal, Verity. You're not only very attractive, but practical and clever, and I admit freely you could be a great deal of help to me.'

Verity turned bright, cold eyes on his watchful face. 'Are you offering me a job?'

Ben stared at her, exasperated. 'No! I'm asking you to marry me.'

She nodded dully. 'I rather thought you were.'

There was a tense silence. Both of them sat very still, each holding an untouched mug of coffee. Verity looked younger than usual in a dress of pink-and-white striped cotton, its dropped waist and demure round collar a contrast to the tailored sophistication of most of her clothes. Warily she cast a look at Ben, who was waiting for her to make some kind of response. He too looked different, his black linen trousers and white shirt conventional enough, but something in their combination with curling black hair giving him the look of an elegant brigand.

'The idea obviously doesn't appeal,' he said at last.

Verity's chin lifted. 'I don't see how you thought it would!'

'Why?'

'Why!' She turned to him angrily. 'You may look on marriage as a business proposition, but I don't. I wouldn't choose a husband merely because he's well-qualified for the post; I'd need—want—something much more than that.' She calmed down a little, adding, 'What exactly would be required from me if I accepted?'

'A child,' said Ben curtly. 'Otherwise *I*'m the one bestowing the worldly goods.'

Verity looked away. 'I see. From the way you put it I rather felt you wanted me to run the estate for you.'

'Thank you, no.' Ben was offended, and for once showed it. 'With the help of a farm manager my father does that, and as soon as I'm able to I shall take over. My view was that your involvement in land management would provide us both with a great deal more common interest than most couples.' He stared at his coffee mug blankly as though he had no idea how it came to be in his hand, and Verity relieved him of it, glad of something to do as she put it down with her own on a table. Ben frowned and began again. 'My parents are getting rather insistent on the subject of a wife, and I feel sure you're exactly the type of woman they have in mind. To me you seem the logical choice, and frankly I don't see why you should be upset.'

'I can see that,' said Verity sadly. 'I'm sorry. The answer is no.'

Ben jumped to his feet and stood with legs apart, staring down at her, his brows meeting in a face less deadpan than usual. Verity met his hostile look with a composure that hid her inner quaking.

'Am I allowed to ask why? he asked, with considerable control.

'We don't know each other well enough,' she said colourlessly. This was the merest tip of her iceberg of reasons, but she felt disinclined to explain further.

'A deficit soon remedied,' he said at once.

'I don't think it would make any difference.' To her dismay Verity gave an involuntary little yawn, due to nerves more than weariness.

Ben turned on his heel. 'I'll say good night, Verity, before I bore you to death.'

'No, please.' She sprang up and put a detaining hand on his arm. 'Let me explain.' She smiled up into his taut face persuasively, and after a moment's hesitation he sat in the chair opposite, where he could watch her face. 'I don't *want* to get married, Ben,' she went on. 'At least not at the moment. And when I do I feel it should be for reasons other than those you put forward. I don't want to be asked because I'm sensible and capable and look as though I'll breed easily. No—please let me go on.' Ben stirred restlessly but let her continue, his eyes brooding. 'I love my work,' explained Verity, 'and I like being my own mistress—no innuendo intended. Not only that, I don't really match up to you socially. My father was a chartered surveyor, like me, and in her youth my mother was a teacher, so my pedigree is rather more plebeian than yours.'

'Rubbish,' interrupted Ben rudely. 'As if it mattered two hoots these days!'

'But you'll have a title one day——'

'So what! I'm still the same man. Me, Benedict Dysart, ex-Marine, more fitted for wargames than anything else, I grant you. Oh to hell with this.' He jumped to his feet and strode to the door. 'Just forget the whole thing, Verity. It seemed like a good idea to me. I'm only sorry you don't agree. Good night.'

Verity ran after him into the hall. 'Don't go off like this, Ben.'

Scowling he shook off the hand she laid on his arm, for once shaken out of his usual impassivity.

'There's no point in my hanging on. I'm just wasting my time—and yours.'

'Oh very well,' she snapped, eyes flashing. 'If you're set on being so childish and unreasonable it's best you do go.'

They glared at each other in silence, until a corner of Ben's mouth unexpectedly began to twitch, the look in his eyes gradually changing from fury to laughter. Unwillingly Verity's mouth curved in an answering smile.

'We sound like a couple of schoolkids,' he said. 'Who the hell would *want* to marry a morose swine like me anyway!'

'Nearly every other female of my acquaintance I should think.' Verity put out a hand to touch his and his own closed round it instantly. 'There are hundreds of girls who would stampede into your arms if you gave them the slightest encouragement as you very well know.'

'But not you, Verity?' The laughter faded, and slowly something more electric took its place, charging the atmosphere between them. Ben released her hand and held out his arms. 'Why not make the experiment yourself, Verity—if only in the interest of research?'

Verity's eyes dropped to hide the unsuspected spark that ignited deep within her at the caressing note in the normally abrasive voice. Ben's hands remained a hair's breadth away as she leaned against the banister, and unbidden her body moved the necessary fraction to make contact with the long, hard fingers that closed on her bare arms and pulled her towards him, giving her all the time in the world to draw away. Curiosity, and some other less-defined emotion, took her forward into his embrace, directing her mouth upwards as his came down to meet it. As Ben's mouth touched hers his arms closed around her, and the option to stay or retreat was no longer open. There was no sudden assault as on that other time. None was necessary. Verity was as eager for the embrace as Ben, her body yielding gladly to the pressure that brought her close against six foot of thinly clad flesh, bone and muscle. Several minutes ticked by on the grandfather clock in the hall while they gave themselves up to the sheer pleasure of contact, mouth to mouth and body to body in the vibrating silence, until Ben eventually raised his head to stare down into her face, his breathing uneven.

'You see?' An audible tremor in his voice matched the vibration deep inside Verity. 'The arrangement would *not* be entirely businesslike, would it?'

'No.' Her eyes were honest as they met his. 'That doesn't mean I've changed my mind though, Ben.'

He gave her an odd, indulgent little smile as he stood back and held out his hand. 'Walk me to the gate, Verity.'

'Rephrase your request,' she said bluntly and stayed where she was.

'*Please* walk me to the gate, Verity,' he said promptly and pounced, catching her hand. 'Come on, do as you're told!'

Laughing together they strolled down the path, meeting a weary Henrietta on her way home from the theatre. Introductions were made, Henrietta's curious eyes examining Ben in the light from the street lamp as they exchanged pleasantries for a short while before she took herself indoors.

'Pretty girl, from what I could see,' commented Ben as he opened the gate. 'Tactful, too.'

'Why?' asked Verity.

'She went off in a hurry,' he explained with exaggerated patience, 'because she thought I wanted to kiss you good night. And she was right.'

Verity deftly avoided his seeking arms, her eyes dancing.

'One swallow doesn't make a summer, Mr Dysart!'

Ben sighed regretfully, his teeth showing white as he smiled, but he made no attempt to dissuade her.

'Pity! Good night, Verity.' With a casual wave he folded himself into the Morgan and departed.

Henrietta was waiting in the kitchen, her face bright with curiosity. 'I say, Vee, was *that* your pedigree chum?'

Verity chuckled. 'You could put it more gracefully, but yes, that was Benedict Dysart in the flesh.'

'More like sheer muscle to me, darling, and from what I could see not in the least aristocratic!' Henrietta gave a little wriggle and perched on the kitchen table while Verity made coffee. 'I mean, he's not exactly effete and chinless, is he? That knee-trembling glimpse I had of him having his wicked way with you in that earthy looking get-up wasn't misleading a bit.' To her surprise Verity flushed bright scarlet.

'He was *not* having his way with me,' stated Verity firmly and took a gulp of coffee. 'And no doubt his physique is due to his training in the Marines—in a Commando Brigade I think.'

'Oh don't go on,' implored Henrietta. 'There's you with all that overdose of machismo on your hands, and the bloke who brought me home was only interested in his new haircut and the fit of his tights in the play tonight!'

'Go to bed,' ordered Verity, grinning. 'You look tired, Hett.'

Henrietta obediently slid off the table and made for the door. She turned with a sly gleam in her big blue eyes.

'Whereas you, darling landlady, look positively blooming. Can it be love?' She sank in a graceful obeisance somewhat at odds with her faded jeans, and made her exit with all the éclat of a budding Peggy Ashcroft.

Laughing, Verity washed coffee mugs, then wandered into the garden to put the loungers in the garage. Henrietta was fun to have around, she would miss her at the end of the season. By then Jenny would be married, and new tenants for the rooms upstairs would have to be found. The scent of newly cut grass hung in the air as Verity went slowly back across the lawn; she felt restless and wide-awake, leaning against the open kitchen door for some time, gazing at the stars, unwilling to admit that Henrietta's last sally had raised a question Verity found difficult to answer. Ben's proposal had been unsatisfactory because she wanted something couched in more romantic terms, if she were honest. Love-songs and deeds of derring do, or even physical attentions pressed on her at every turn were all unnecessary. But a proposal made merely because she was attractive and sensible and likely to prove fertile was rather like a rub down with a wet sponge.

The more Verity considered it the less easy she found it to define her feelings towards Ben. At first she'd despised him, then learned to tolerate him, and for the past couple of weeks she had enjoyed his company without reservation. Well, perhaps one reservation, namely Gussie. No one ever described Gussie as merely attractive or sensible. Beautiful, luscious, stunning, perhaps, but girls who looked like Gussie weren't expected to be sensible. Verity frowned and bit her lip. Perhaps she herself wasn't quite as level-headed as she imagined—the very thought of Ben's kiss was enough to shake her faith in her own immunity. She rather suspected good old-fashioned lust had caught up with her at last—certainly not love.

This thought remained with her all through a busy Sunday taken up with household chores and gardening, right up to mid-day on Monday when she emerged from John Randall's office to run straight into Ben.

'Come and have lunch,' he said, and smiled straight into her startled eyes, reviving the sensations in her midriff first experienced two nights before.

'No,' said Verity bluntly, and promptly bolted for her office, to the surprise of both receptionists, who were looking on with interest. With a lazy, conspiratorial look at the two girls Ben strolled after Verity, his indolence dropping from him like a cloak as he wrenched open her office door, closing it behind him with a quiet care that affected Verity more than if he'd slammed it shut.

Verity sat bolt upright in her swivel chair, looking at him with a mixture of resentment and apprehension. He put his weight on the palms of his hands on her desk and leaned across it, his face coldly questioning.

'Why the hell did you scuttle away like that? We provided a very interesting spectacle.'

Verity shrugged. 'I don't want to have lunch with you.'

'Fine. It's a free country. But why dash off as though I was about to attack you?'

'I have work to do,' she said pointedly and took up her pen.

Ben's face relaxed and he straightened. 'What's the matter, Verity? Afraid of the big bad wolf?'

'No. I just think it better if we don't see each other any more.'

'Are you afraid I'll keep on proposing?' he asked dryly.

Verity's fear was more that she'd accept, and for all the wrong reasons. 'Something like that, Ben.'

'I see.' Ben ran a hand through his hair, frowning. 'If I promise never to mention marriage again, would that make things better?'

To Verity's dismay it made things infinitely worse. 'To me you're still Gussie's property,' she said with brutal frankness. 'You'd be better off with someone who doesn't know her, or know what relationship you both enjoyed when you were younger. No woman likes to feel she's a substitute.'

'You make it sound more like a football match than a marriage.' To Verity's surprise Ben took her statement with unexpected equanimity. 'Why not lunch with me, Verity, and let's talk this over. After that I promise I'll leave you in peace. If you want me to.'

With misgivings Verity consented, and preceded Ben through the back corridor to the car park, glad to avoid the interested faces in the front reception area. She got in the Morgan silently and sat staring ahead of her, hardly noticing where they were going until she realised they were on the road for Priorsford.

'Where are you taking me?' she demanded.

'Home.'

'Temple Priors?' Verity squeaked. 'Why for heaven's sake! Your parents will hardly be pleased to have a lunch guest unexpectedly, and in any case I'm not dressed for visiting. Please take me back.'

'If you'll just be quiet for a second,' he said calmly, 'my parents went to Stowe earlier, and I told Martha, the cook, to make sandwiches for us. I just want to show you over the house.' He gave a glance at her pink shirt and pleated brown linen skirt. 'You look fine to me.'

Verity was not consoled. She fumed in silence as the car skirted the village of Priorsford and followed the road for three miles before turning through gates to wind down a drive that led through pastures full of sleek Jersey cows before a dip in the road brought the house into view. Seeming to grow out of its surrounding landscape, its steep gables and chimneys rose weathered and beautiful to command the eye even before the building came fully into view. As Ben stopped the car Verity gazed at the lichened stone tiles of a roof that had sheltered Dysarts for four centuries, impressed as she'd known she would be, yet drawn irresistibly by the charm of many-paned windows that reflected the sunlight and the arched, weathered door that stood open in welcome.

Ben said nothing as he helped her out of the car, merely taking her hand to lead her through the doorway into a square, sizeable hall, its dark floor gleaming with the lustre of well-polished wood. Verity had no eyes for the floor. The entire hall was dominated by a great stone fireplace over which hung a portrait of a man in the clothes of the early seventeenth century. She walked slowly towards it, other portraits on the panelled walls fading into insignificance beside the impact of the man staring down at her from the great gilded frame on the chimney breast. The black, curling hair was longer, a gold ring glinted in one ear and a great emerald on the hand that caressed the head of an Irish wolfhound, but otherwise it was Ben.

'A relation of yours?' asked Verity, without turning her head.

'Nicholas Dysart. He built the place.'

Verity continued to gaze at the portrait, a slight frown creasing her forehead.

'What is it?' asked Ben, watching her.

She turned to look at him, a withdrawn little smile on her lips, and gestured at their surroundings, then up at the portrait.

'All this, especially *him*, rather point up the difference between us. The most I could produce in the same line would be a few sepia-tinted photographs of my great-grandparents in the albums Mother left at home.'

Ben took her elbow and drew her down beside him on the settle beside the fireplace. 'Everyone has to start somewhere, Verity.' He jerked a finger towards the portrait. 'His only claim to aristocracy was sheer audacity. He managed to seduce the daughter of a wealthy wool merchant, who with reluctance handed both the lady and her dowry to the wily Nick, enabling him to build this house, and put up the necessary money to buy a baronetcy from James I. The going rate at the time in 1611 was the cost of thirty soldiers to serve in Ireland for three years, and not only did the social-climbing Nick provide the ready, but he sent off his younger brother—Benedict, of course, of whom he was less than fond—to serve with them, in the hope that he'd be bumped off.'

Verity stared at him suspiciously. 'You're pulling my leg!'

Ben shook his head, grinning. 'Not a bit of it. The joke was that by 1618 King James was so chronically hard up he dropped the asking price for a baronetcy to £220, and any old riff-raff could buy one, which caused no end of an outcry among Sir Nick and his ilk, as you can imagine.'

'Nevertheless, I am deeply impressed,' insisted Verity.

'Because we've been here a long time! What I'm trying to stress is that there was precious little breeding or merit in that ruffian up there,' Ben said persistently.

'You look just like him,' said Verity dryly.

'A vulgar ruffian, you mean. Thanks!' Ben stood up, pulling her with him as an elderly woman in a flowered overall emerged from a door at the back of the hall. Two dogs came hurtling after her, skidding on the polished boards to greet Ben with as much fuss as though it were days, instead of hours, since parted from him.

'Martha,' said Ben. 'This is Miss Verity Marsh, from Lockhart & Welch. Verity, this is Mrs Baines—head cook and bottle washer.'

The woman's plump face creased in a smile of welcome. 'Pleased to meet you, Miss Verity.'

'How do you do, Mrs Baines.' Verity smiled warmly and held out her hand. The woman took it, pleased.

'Just Martha, Miss. Now where do you want your lunch, Mr Ben?'

'In the morning room, Martha, please. I'll take Verity on a tour of the house, so give us half an hour.' Ben took Verity's arm, shooing away the two retrievers.

'I'll be late getting back——' began Verity.

'I cleared it with John beforehand.'

An eyebrow raised at his high-handedness, Verity followed Ben up the wide staircase at the end of the hall, privately thinking he looked very much in keeping with his surroundings as he led her through a series of surprisingly comfortable bedrooms, only one possessing the expected fourposter.

'This room is kept for show, everything in it dating from when the house was built.' Ben flicked at the bedhangings. 'Nothing would induce my mother to sleep in a fourposter bed, she's always convinced the top will collapse in on her in the night.'

Oddly reassured by this snippet of information, Verity peeped into several more rooms, the smallest and most spartan of which she found belonged to Ben.

'Do you ever open the house to the public?' she asked as they returned downstairs.

'Too small. There'd be no place for us to go.'

On the ground floor the hall took up a great deal of the space, the rest given to a formal drawing-room with brocade-covered furniture, more pictures, and pieces of fragile porcelain scattered round on inlaid tables, a surprisingly functional dining-room with quantities of silver on the massive oak sideboard, a book-lined study, hearteningly untidy, and finally a small, cheerful sitting-room cosy with chintz and flower prints, where lunch awaited them on a low table.

'We'll leave the kitchen and the outbuildings to another day,' said Ben, to Verity's relief, and waved her to a seat at the tray, where she poured hot fragrant coffee from a silver pot and accepted wafer-thin sandwiches of rare roast beef from the plate Ben proffered.

'Well?' he demanded.

'Are you asking if I like your home?' Verity took an experimental bite of her sandwich without looking at him.

'And do you?'

'It's very beautiful—much more lived-in than I expected.'

'We *do* live in it.'

'But with only your parents to occupy such a large house, why should you need another for yourself?' she asked curiously.

Ben was quiet for a time. 'Nick's health was never good,' he said at last. 'I always knew that I was the one expected to marry and produce an heir, archaic as it sounds, but since Nick died I agree with my parents. It's time I found a wife.'

'A pity the lady of your choice had married someone else in the meantime.' It was out before Verity could stop herself, but Ben merely gave her rather an austere look and ignored her comment, not even troubling to deny it.

'When I do marry,' he went on, 'I'd prefer a place of my own to start with—wouldn't you agree?'

'Then what was the object of showing me all this?' Verity waved an arm towards the open French windows and the view of the terrace and gardens beyond.

'My intention was to introduce you by degrees to my background, as you insist on considering it so different from yours. I thought I'd show you the house first, introduce you to my parents some other time and finally come round to the basics. In other words, could you contemplate living in Tern Cottage with me, knowing it had once belonged to Gussie.' Ben sat back in his chair and waited for Verity to answer, his face expressionless. Deliberately Verity poured herself more coffee and drank most of it before answering.

'The house, to be honest, is certainly a little awe-inspiring,' she said honestly. 'Your parents I haven't met yet, but my feelings about Tern Cottage are very cut and dried. Covetous describes them best, I think.' Verity held up a hand as Ben sat up straight, a gleam of triumph in his eyes. 'But you're missing the point somewhere, Ben. None of these things has any bearing on your proposition. I use the word advisedly,' she added. 'No proposal should be so businesslike if it wants to succeed.'

'I thought it best to lay my cards on the table,' he said. 'My idea was that if you can swallow the trappings that go with me I'm confident I can overcome your misgivings about the rest, given time.'

Verity sighed, unconvinced. 'Why me? The surrounding countryside must be literally awash with well-bred maidens panting to marry such an eligible prospect, every last one of them infinitely more suitable than me!'

'I wouldn't know,' he said indifferently. 'I'm only concerned with my own choice; which is you.' His eyes narrowed. 'It seems to disturb you that I've approached the whole idea with my head, rather than that less reliable organ the heart. Am I right?'

'I hadn't really given it much thought,' lied Verity.

Ben looked sceptical. 'When you do find time to give it some consideration at least you need have no qualms about the physical side of the union, after our illuminating little encounter the other night.'

'There isn't going to *be* any union, as you so delicately put it.' Verity glanced at her watch. 'I won't have a job soon, unless I get back to it fairly soon. Will you drive me back to town please?' As she got up the door opened to admit the excited retrievers, and close behind them two people who could only be Ben's parents, to Verity's dismay.

Slim and youthful, with greying fair hair, Ben's mother came swiftly towards Verity, a smile on her attractive face as she held out her hand.

'You must be Verity Marsh,' said Lady Dysart

warmly. 'I'm so happy to meet you my dear, Ben says you've been very helpful to him.'

'How do you do, Lady Dysart.' Verity took the outstretched hand, smiling politely.

'My husband Hugh,' said Isabel Dysart blithely.

There was a strong resemblance between father and son, even to the glint in Sir Hugh's eye as he took Verity's hand, his head on one side as he studied her flushed face. 'By the centre, I never met a surveyor who looked like you—small wonder Ben was so eager to get into Stratford every morning.' He laughed, and clapped his son on his shoulder.

Lady Dysart fixed him with a disapproving eye. 'You're making Verity blush, Hugh.' She smiled at Verity kindly. 'I hope Martha gave you a good lunch—so tiresome of Ben to insist on bringing you today when we had to be in Stowe, but we cut our visit short in the hope of catching you.'

'Verity's a very busy lady. She can't always spare the time,' said Ben, avoiding Verity's eye. 'You only just caught us—she's anxious to get back to the grindstone.'

'Yes, of course. Never mind, you must come again soon when we can spend more time together.' Lady Dysart patted Verity's hand.

Inwardly dismayed Verity took her leave, apologising for having to rush away, keeping silent in the Morgan until Temple Priors was out of sight. As soon as they were on the main road she turned to Ben angrily.

'Your parents knew you were bringing me to lunch.'

Ben nodded coolly. 'Yes, of course.'

'Didn't they think it odd—my coming on a day they were out?'

'Not in the least. I told them I wanted to show you over the place on our own for the first time—which is the simple truth.' Ben put out a hand and touched Verity's. She snatched it away.

'What reason did you give?'

'Once again the truth. I told them I intend to marry you.'

CHAPTER SIX

BEN'D unshakable conviction on the subject of their
eventual marriage made Verity's life difficult, she
found. It was useless refusing to see him. He dogged her
footsteps so persistently at the office the entire
workforce of Lockhart & Welch was agog with
curiosity, to the point of taking bets on the outcome, to
Verity's disgust when John Randall told her about it.

'Put them out of their misery, Verity,' he said,
grinning. 'No one is concentrating on their work in
their interest. *Are* you two heading for the altar?'

'I can't answer for Mr Dysart,' she answered shortly,
'but I most certainly am not.'

'He now legally owns Tern Cottage, you know,' John
said slyly.

'Really. Shall we get on?' Verity's expression was so
forbidding her employer gave up and turned to the
business of the day.

Alone in the house the next evening Verity was
absorbed in a play on television when the doorbell rang.
Frowning she went to the door, neither surprised nor
pleased to see Ben.

'I was passing,' he said, deadpan. 'I thought I'd drop
in.'

Without a word Verity stood aside and waved him
into the sitting-room, switching off the television set.

'Coffee?' she asked.

'No thanks, just a friendly chat.' He sat down on the
sofa, catching her hand to pull her down beside him.
She resisted angrily.

'This has got to stop, Ben!'

'What has?' He leaned back comfortably, a look of
infuriating innocence in his eyes.

'You know very well.' Verity thrust an impatient

99

hand through her heavy hair. 'I'm tired of knowing glances at work, to be precise. I learnt yesterday that they're making a book on how soon our wedding takes place. I want it to stop, Ben. I mean it.'

He shrugged his heavy shoulders. 'I haven't said a word.'

'You don't have to.' She glared at him. 'It's the way you behave. Do you have to be everywhere I am all the time? It's driving me mad.'

Ben put out a hand to smooth her ruffled hair. 'Never mind; only another two days and you'll be rid of me—at the office, at least.'

Verity was diverted. 'Learned enough already?'

'I don't suppose I'll ever know *enough*, but I think the time has come to try and lighten Father's load.' Ben sobered. 'His health was affected considerably by the shock of Nick's death. His blood pressure's worrying my mother no end, so it's time I pitched in and lent a hand.'

Almost guilty at the relief she felt, Verity smiled sympathetically. 'I'm sorry your father's not well, but at the same time I can't help thinking that with you gone perhaps all this ridiculous speculation about us will die down.'

Ben's mouth twisted in an ironic smile. 'You might at least pretend a little polite regret at my departure.'

Verity got up. 'I find it hard to dissemble, Mr Dysart. Can I get you a drink? There's some beer in the fridge.'

'Thank you.'

When Verity returned with a glass tankard of beer for her guest she sat on the floor, her back to the armchair opposite Ben. With her long legs in tight, worn denim and her hair tied up in a loose knot on top of her head she looked very different from the efficient young surveyor of earlier in the day.

'You look good in jeans,' he said.

Verity glanced up in amusement, and changed the subject, giving an airy wave at their surroundings.

'Suitable attire for *my* home, Ben, but hardly fitting for the more stately residence you live in.'

'Are you a snob, Verity?'

'Inverted variety you mean,' she said quickly, flushing. 'No, I don't think so. It just suddenly struck me what a contrast this is in every way to our little lunch together at your place.'

Ben put down the tankard and leaned forward, his hands clasped between his knees.

'If I were some chap from down the road would it make you more amenable to the thought of marrying me, Verity? Is it just my damn background that's sticking in your throat?'

Verity met his eyes honestly. 'No. That has no bearing at all.'

His jaw clenched. 'Then why, Verity? Why won't you marry me?'

Because you don't love me, she thought, and I don't . . . Her mind went blank and the colour faded from her face. She swallowed with difficulty, a shiver running through her.

'What is it?' Ben said urgently. He slid down on his knees beside her and took her hands in his. 'You're cold! Shall I light the fire?'

'No.' She smiled at him with an effort. 'Footsteps on my grave, that's all.' She turned her head away from the black, searching eyes, and experimented with a careless little laugh, a breathless, hoarse little sound that deepened Ben's concern. He picked her up, sitting back on the couch, holding her like a child across his knees, her head turned into his shoulder.

Verity lay passively, knowing she should get up, move about, offer him another drink, anything rather than stay tamely where she was, and after a few moments she sat up, but he pulled her back.

'Stay put for a minute.'

Verity submitted meekly to the comfort of an embrace she knew she was enjoying far too much.

'I'm sorry,' she said. 'Perhaps I'm coming down

with a cold—I got wet in that shower at lunch time today.'

'Don't apologise.' Ben's breath stirred her hair, his voice vibrating under her cheek as she lay against him. 'It's not often I get this close. Are you always so elusive? A kiss or two is admissible even in a friendly relationship, you know, or do your other men friends submit tamely to a veto on all physical contact?'

It was the impetus Verity needed. She detached herself from his hold and stood up, shaking back her hair. 'My other friendships are my affair. Would you care for another beer?'

'No.' Ben held out his arms, a cajoling smile on his face. 'Come back.'

She shook her head, grinning. 'Do you think I'm stupid, Mr Dysart? It's no good flashing your smile at me like that, all it'll get you is another beer.'

Ben was suddenly serious. 'What was the matter, Verity? You changed colour dramatically. Does the idea of marrying me actually make you ill?'

'No. It wasn't that at all.'

'Then what was it?'

'I just felt weird for a moment—nothing more, really.'

'You're lying,' he said flatly.

Verity sat down in the armchair. 'A fuss over nothing. Let's change the subject.'

'No. Let's keep to the point in question. Why won't you marry me?'

Verity sighed wearily. 'Ben, there's no point in going on with this. You know as well as I do that even when the two people involved are madly in love a great many marriages fail. What possible chance of success would there be for us, entering into it like a business transaction?'

'A great deal more,' said Ben positively. 'I can give you a home you've always coveted, security, not to mention liking and respect. In return you can be of tremendous help to me with your training, I admit it freely. You could be a helpmeet, to use an old-fashioned word, to a much larger extent than most wives.'

'I wouldn't have to marry you to do that,' she pointed out quickly. 'I could just come and work for you.'

'You're missing the point.' He leaned forward, his eyes urgent. 'I want a family, Verity, and not just to carry on the name—daughters, sons, it doesn't matter a damn which. It was down there in the South Atlantic that it came home to me just how much I'd missed by not having a wife and children.' He held out a peremptory hand. 'Come and sit here beside me, Verity—please.'

Verity left her chair and did as he asked, yielding to the arm he slid round her to hold her close.

'This is something I've never told anyone,' he went on, 'but I can pinpoint the exact moment. We were deployed on Mount Challenger, about seven miles short of Stanley. It was pitch dark and freezing, and our objective was to take Mount Harriet and Goat Ridge, two hills with outcrops of rock shielding machine-gun nests. Advancing up Harriet was a slow, bloody business. I won't harrow you with the details, but when dawn broke and we knew Harriet was ours all I could feel was a vague, impersonal surprise. I was alive! It was then I realised that what I wanted most out of this rather unexpected gift of life was a wife, family, continuity——' Ben smiled down into Verity's absorbed face. 'Am I making sense?'

'Very much so,' she said, deeply moved. 'It's just that I don't think——'

'Then stop thinking for once,' he said roughly. 'Just feel, Verity, for God's sake just feel!' And he turned her in his arms, kissing her deeply, the pressure of his mouth bending her head back, her body almost prone as he held it prisoner beneath his.

Verity tore her mouth away, breathing hard and shaking her head.

'No, please——' she gasped, and Ben groaned, burying his face in her hair.

'Why is it always no, Verity? Your body and your mouth are saying yes—admit it!' He raised his head and at the molten look in his eyes Verity's breath quickened and the tip of her tongue flicked out to moisten suddenly dry lips. 'Don't!' he said, torment in his voice as his mouth closed on her own, his tongue meeting hers in twisting frenzy as one hand began to caress the curves of her shoulders, running down her spine to encircle her waist and move upward until it found her breasts.

The frantic beating of her heart threatened to shake Verity to pieces as his mouth left hers to roam over her face and down her throat, always returning to her parted lips to tantalise and tease, rousing a deep desire in her for something more as heat surged through her body, dissolving her defences, making nonsense of all her denials.

'Well?' he demanded hotly. 'Tell me you feel nothing, tell me you're immune. Can you, Verity?' He laid his hand on her breast, where her heart-beat clamoured against his palm. Without a word he took her hand and thrust it through his opened shirt, holding it flat against his chest to feel the surging throb of his own heart. 'To take up your argument about common ground,' he said, his voice rough and unsteady, 'can you deny the mutual desire we both feel equally at this very moment?'

Verity stared up into the eyes so close to hers and shook her head unwillingly. 'No, I can't.'

Ben chuckled and sat up, pulling her with him, but still keeping one arm close about her waist. 'That's one denial I *am* pleased to hear. Don't you agree it would contribute towards a successful marriage?'

Verity frowned. 'Surely there should be more to marriage than that!'

Ben let out an explosive breath. 'There would be, you maddening creature! What we just experienced was pure chemistry, I admit, which is all some people ever have as common ground. But in our case there would be mutual liking and respect, the common interest of running the estate, enjoyment of each other's company—by day and by night. God, Verity, what more do you want?'

'Time, Ben.' Sanity and calm were Verity's once more, to her relief. She moved away from him, detached and businesslike, as though the heated moments just before had never happened. 'I shall go up to Birkenhead to my mother at the weekend, and in the meantime I shall give the idea careful thought. Alone. I can hardly be expected to make a rather momentous decision like this in an instant just because, well, it seems the physical side of marriage would present no problem.'

'That's one way of putting it,' he agreed, amused. 'When do I get my answer?'

'When I come back.'

'Will your mother's opinion influence your decision?' he asked.

'I very much doubt if she would go as far as saying "do" or "don't". My mother expects me to make my own decisions.'

Ben stood up. 'Will you kiss me goodnight, at least—perhaps when you come home your answer will be negative, whereupon I shall never darken your door again.'

Verity got to her feet, looking at him thoughtfully. 'You mean if I say no, that's it. You drop me.'

'I wouldn't put it quite like that, but in essence, yes, I would.' Ben took her by the shoulders, his face stern. 'I could never be satisfied with half a loaf, Verity.' He kissed her hard and went, leaving her standing in the middle of the room, her face blank. After a minute or two she went into her bedroom and picked up the telephone.

'Hello, Mother—yes, I'm fine. And you?' They chatted for a few minutes before Verity came to the point. 'How would you like a visitor for the weekend?

Me, of course. Great. Friday night, then. Give Stepdaddy my love. Bye.'

The drive up the M6 on the Friday evening was a test for the concentration, all three lanes full of traffic and the usual obstacle course of roadworks at various points. Verity was tired when she finally arrived at the Craigs' home, a solid. Edwardian house on the outskirts of Birkenhead. As the Mini turned into the drive the front door of the house opened and Hannah Craig flew down the steps to hug her daughter as Verity unfolded her long legs and stood up, stretching and smiling. Her mother was approaching fifty, too rapidly in her own opinion, but looked far less, only an odd strand of grey in hair otherwise as thick and brown as Verity's. She stood at arm's length, her brown eyes searching as she looked her daughter up and down.

'Good journey?'

'Very slow, Mother. No need to ask how you are, younger every time I see you.' Verity kissed her parent fondly, then looked up with a warm smile as she saw Ian Craig waiting to add his welcome. 'Hello, Stepdaddy.'

'Hello, Verity.' Ian Craig was very tall, enough to tower over his stepdaughter, his kind face and friendly grey eyes alight with warmth as he gave Verity a kiss. 'About time you tore yourself away from your wheeling and dealing. Your mother tends to pine if you stay away too long.'

'So I see.' Verity gave a mocking glance at her mother's healthy, tanned face. 'No doubt you cane her regularly, like your students, to produce that wan effect?'

'Perhaps I haven't exactly pined,' said Hannah, urging Verity towards the house, 'but I would like to see you a little more often.'

'Leave her in peace until she's eaten,' advised Ian. 'Knowing Verity I'll lay odds she's starving.'

For once Verity proved him wrong. She did her best

with the fresh salmon and green peas her mother served, but the latter's sharp eyes grew more and more thoughtful as Verity fiddled with only a token portion of her favourite apricot soufflé, and afterwards refused cheese in favour of several cups of black coffee.

Ian lectured in maths at a local college of further education, and occasionally did some private coaching at home, so excused himself after dinner when one of his pupils arrived for tuition.

'We'll leave the dishes for the moment,' said Hannah firmly. 'Want a brandy? Liqueur?'

Verity shook her head, knowing the moment of truth had arrived. Her mother's antennae were patently working overtime.

'What's the problem, babe?' asked Hannah bluntly. 'A man?'

Verity smiled. 'If I do have a problem, why should you think it's a man?'

Her mother shrugged and lit a cigarette. 'Call it maternal intuition. You sort your own problems out very efficiently as a rule, education, job, paying-guests and so on. So now I think it must be something different, and my bones tell me it's a man. Is it this Niall Gordon you've mentioned?'

'No. In fact Niall is at present in a state of high dungeon because I've been seeing someone else.'

Hannah's eyes narrowed through the cigarette smoke. 'Have you now. Who?'

Verity spread her hands with a wry, helpless little gesture. 'I've been an idiot, Mother. Somehow or other I've managed to get involved with an old flame of Gussie Middleton's.'

'I wouldn't have thought you two shared the same taste, darling.' Hannah stubbed out her cigarette, carefully avoiding her daughter's eyes. 'I seem to remember she had some wild affair with that Dysart boy from Temple Priors—the one who went into the Marines.'

'Got it in one, Mother.'

They looked at each other for a moment.

'How involved is involved?' asked Hannah casually.

'He wants me to marry him.' Verity grinned as her mother let out an inelegant whistle. 'His brother Nicholas died in a fire last year and Ben is now out of the Marines, his sights on a suitable wife to produce an heir to the title—and for some reason he seems to think I fill the bill.'

'I agree with him there, naturally.' Hannah smiled questioningly. 'How do you feel about it?'

'I don't know.' Verity coloured and looked away. 'What I mean, Mother dear, is that I'm not sure what I feel about *marrying* Ben. I suddenly discovered how I feel about the man himself the other day—which is more or less why I'm here.'

'I'm very glad you are—but slightly in the dark as to what's bothering you. He wants to marry you, and you implied that you're in love with him. So where's the obstacle?'

Verity got up restlessly and moved to the window, looking out blindly into the garden.

'The thing is, I'm greedy,' she said bitterly. 'I want the lot. Sensible, level-headed Verity, who always found the idea of heated emotions rather embarrassing.'

Hannah smiled tenderly at her tall daughter's averted profile. 'And now it isn't.'

'No. Ben considers that our mutual liking and the interests we have in common, not to mention my profession, are a much better basis for marriage than any *grande passion*, whereas I want him on his knees, laying his heart and soul at my feet on a plate, as well as all his worldly goods.' Verity swung round. 'He *likes* me, that's obvious, and, well, there's no problem about the physical side either——'

'Which is a help!'

Verity smiled unwillingly.

'As you say, Mother. Well? I've come to consult the oracle. You've been married twice, and each time very successfully, so tell me what to do. Marry him and hope that in time his feelings hot up a bit, or turn him down and let him find some other suitable candidate?'

Hannah began clearing the table. 'If your Ben's going about the whole thing in such a businesslike way it rather surprises me that he *does* consider you so eligible.'

'Thanks!' Verity grinned as she helped.

'No, seriously darling, his parents must surely have hoped their son would marry into some local family with a background like theirs. There's nothing very aristocratic about us, love. Respectable, but a bit lacking in the old blue blood.'

'Ben seems more interested in my land management qualifications than my pedigree,' said Verity candidly. 'And I rather get the impression that since Nick, his brother, died, the Dysarts are more concerned with Ben being happy than anything else.' She sighed. 'The trouble is, Mother, I can't help feeling Ben still hankers a bit after Gussie, deep down. She certainly still hankers after him.'

Hannah Craig hefted the loaded tray and led the way to the kitchen, where they both began to dispose of the washing up.

'Augusta always was a spoilt brat, and obviously hasn't changed in the slightest. It's time she faced up to reality.' Hannah slid the last of the plates in the dishrack and took off her rubber gloves, looking Verity squarely in the eye. 'If you want my opinion, darling, the best thing I can advise is to follow your inclinations. If you want to marry Ben Dysart, marry him. Even if he does feel something still for Gussie, propinquity is a wonderful ally—I'll lay you ten to one you can soon scotch that, or you're no daughter of mine!'

Verity's face cleared and her eyes lit with laughter. 'So that's your considered opinion, Mrs Craig? Marry him and make myself indispensable in all departments?'

'Especially bed,' agreed Hannah promptly.

'Mother, really! Is that the right thing to say to your daughter!'

'You asked for advice, babe, so I'm giving it. Go back to Stratford, say yes to your lordling and I'll start saving up for a frivolous hat.'

Verity reached home late on Sunday evening, just as the streetlamps began to blossom in the twilight. The house was deserted, a note on the kitchen table in Henrietta's idiosyncratic scrawl.

'Jen's in work, I'm out socialising, quiche in fridge. *Two* phone-calls from a CERTAIN PERSON. (Well, well!) Love, H.'

Verity grinned and took her grip into her bedroom, rang her mother, then had a leisurely bath, refusing to leave the warm, scented water when the telephone rang. Some perverse instinct kept her where she was, eyes closed, but as a diversionary tactic it failed somewhat. The ringing began again while she was patting herself dry, and she shrugged into her kimono and went into the bedroom to answer it.

'You've finally come home,' said Ben's voice without greeting.

'Yes.'

'You're late. I've rung you before.'

'I know, I saw the message.'

'Well?' he demanded impatiently. 'What's the answer, yes or no?'

Now that the moment had arrived Verity found it hard to give her consent in cold blood to an impersonal telephone receiver. 'Could we meet tomorrow and talk?' she asked. There was a pause.

'I'll pick you up at twelve-thirty,' he said curtly.

'No—I'm out most of the day. Could you call round tomorrow evening?'

'Eightish then. Good night.' Ben rang off abruptly, leaving her a little deflated. Shrugging, Verity sat on her bed to dry her hair, a lengthy process which normally she found soothing, but tonight her hair crackled with electricity, and the task seemed to take twice as long as usual, getting on her nerves. Her teeth caught her lower lip as her hands went on automatically with their task while her mind worked overtime. In her mother's company the whole thing had seemed so cut and dried. She loved Ben, *ergo* she should marry him. It had never seemed remotely possible to feel like this about any man, let alone someone always looked upon as Gussie's property. Verity clenched her jaw as she remembered all the unwanted information Gussie had insisted on imparting as to how wonderful Ben Dysart was, and how thrilling a lover he could be. Verity bent her head to her knees to brush her hair forward from root to tip, willing the angry, hard strokes to banish all remembrance of those long ago whispered revelations in the dark.

Verity switched off the hair-dryer but remained for long moments with her head on her knees, her hair hanging down, facing the fact that she wanted to be Ben Dysart's wife at all costs, regardless of the difference in their backgrounds, or even of the fact that he might still be in love with Gussie. Her mother was dead right. Verity Marsh would just have to make sure that there was no room in Benedict Dysart's life for any other woman. She threw back her head and gave a scream of fright as Ben Dysart appeared in the doorway, almost as if conjured up by the vehemence of her mental vow.

'I rang the doorbell,' he said, as Verity stared up at him wordlessly. 'There was no answer, but the kitchen door was open yet again, so I came in.'

In the muted light from the bedside lamp he looked angry and threatening, no gleam of white teeth to break the darkness of his face as he looked at her accusingly.

'I came in through the front door, I didn't check to see if the other one was locked.' Her explanation sounded lame, and Verity felt irritated that she had need to make it.

'If you leave doors unlocked,' he said harshly, 'and lights on in your bedroom window, one day someone with more villainous intent than me is going to break in here and do some real harm.'

'After being frightened to death twice I shan't forget another time,' snapped Verity. 'You've made your point.'

Ben came a little further into the room, his face relaxing a little.

'Did you have a good weekend?' he asked with an effort.

'Yes, thank you.' Verity looked at him curiously, noticing for the first time that his hair was wet, and clung in damp curls, flat against his head. 'You're wet, is it raining?'

'No. I rang you from John Randall's round the corner. I've been there to dinner, and had a swim in his pool afterwards.' He smiled for the first time. 'Didn't you think I got here rather quickly?'

'I didn't notice the time.' Verity gave a restless glance at the open door. 'Look, it's late, I'm not dressed and Henrietta may be in at any time, don't you think. . . .' She trailed into silence as Ben shouldered the door shut and leaned against it, arms folded, a mocking smile on his mouth.

'No, Verity, I don't think. I didn't come round here at this time of night to be sent home like a naughty boy. I've come for your answer.'

They stood staring at each other like enemies, hostility and tension crackling in the air between them. Verity felt annoyed. She had no intention of saying yes under these circumstances, in this enforced intimacy. Her chin lifted.

'Ben, please. It's getting late and I'm tired after my trip—I need some sleep. Let's talk tomorrow, as I suggested.'

'All right,' he said off-handedly, taking the wind out of her sails. He came towards her. 'Give me a good night kiss and I'll go.'

Verity eyed him with suspicion, then closed her eyes and offered her mouth with an air of long-suffering.

'Open your eyes,' he commanded.

Her lids flew open, her mouth parting in surprise at his peremptory bark, and at once his mouth was on hers, moving over it persuasively while his arms slid round her, his hands applying pressure on the small of her back so that her body curved involuntarily into his. Suddenly all the hostility seemed childish and unnecessary, as Ben's mouth caressed and kissed not only her mouth, but her throat and her ears, his touch featherlight on her skin as she yielded to him, nestling against his hard body as he buried his face in her hair.

'Are you going to marry me?' he said, his voice muffled.

Verity tipped her head back and looked up at him without prevarication.

'Yes,' she said simply.

He gave an odd little sound, deep in his throat, and kissed her hard, his hands threading through her hair to hold her still beneath the caress, which softened to woo and entice. Verity's lips opened naturally under his, her own hands moving up his shoulders and the taut muscles of his neck to bury themselves in the damp black curls. She felt his body stir with desire against hers and arched herself against him, shamelessly glad when he gasped and pulled her even closer, unconcerned that her robe slackened and fell apart as they twined together. His hands were urgent on her responsive breasts, which hardened and shaped to his touch, the nipples erecting in anticipation of the lips and teeth that kissed and nibbled and tugged, until she was in a frenzy of longing that turned to bitter disappointment as Ben suddenly let her go, turning his back on her and breathing hard as he tucked his shirt back into place and fought for self-control.

Verity wrapped her robe tightly around her, tying the sash with shaking fingers and making vain efforts to smooth down her wayward hair. Ben turned and caught her by the elbows, looking down at her with disturbed eyes.

'I'm sorry,' he said huskily. 'Come into the other room, for God's sake.'

She shook her head.

'Hett will be home in a minute and I don't look very respectable.' Her colour rose as her eyes followed his to the nipples that stood out against the thin cotton of her kimono.

'No,' he agreed gruffly. 'You look——'

'Shameless,' she said flatly, and stooped to pick up her hairbrush.

'Wrong.' He pulled her upright and bent to kiss each taut little peak through the cotton before putting her forcibly from him. 'I'm going, Verity. For reasons obvious to us both. I'll pick you up tomorrow night— make it sevenish though, if you can.'

'Why? Where are we going?'

'Home to dinner with my mother and father, and a trip down to Tern Cottage afterwards where you can tell me how you want it furnished.' He grinned and touched her cheek. 'After all that was where we first met, so it's entirely fitting.'

Verity gave him a cat-like little smile. 'I haven't forgotten anything about that day, believe me!'

Ben frowned, his face abruptly austere. 'Forget about Gussie,' he ordered. 'She belongs to the past. Everyone's entitled to the languishing and sentimentality of calf-love as part of growing up. But you and I have something much better, with so many more things going for us—not least of all this.' Ben kissed her again, lingeringly and explicitly. 'Oh yes,' he breathed, 'most definitely *this*,' and went on kissing her for some time until he literally pushed her away and made for the door.

Verity stood with her fingers against her mouth, staring for some time at her bedroom door after it had closed behind Ben. Eventually she slid her nightgown over her head, subdued her hair to some kind of order and climbed wearily into bed. Well, the deed was done. She had given her promise, and she would keep it. But it was no substitute for what she really wanted. She wanted all the languishing and the sentimentality too, all the frills, a man who not only liked and desired her, but loved her to distraction as well.

CHAPTER SEVEN

'I'M nervous,' said Verity frankly as the Morgan left Stratford the following evening. Ben glanced down at her in amusement and put out a hand to cover hers.

'What would your colleagues say now if they saw the efficient Miss Marsh in a spin over nothing!'

'It may be nothing to you, Ben Dysart, but for me it's a fairly momentous occasion.'

'For me also,' he said emphatically. 'It's not every day of the week I take home a prospective daughter-in-law for my parents.'

'I'm relieved to hear it.' Verity gave him a rueful little grin. 'I feel a bit like the beggar-maid to your King Cophetua—somehow one never hears how she got on with his relatives afterwards.'

Ben chuckled. 'Mine are delighted, Verity, believe me.' He shot a comprehensive glance at her. 'So am I, incidentally. Did I mention that you look extremely attractive tonight? If we weren't a bit late I'd stop somewhere and show you just how suitable *I* think you are. Perhaps you should keep it in mind that it's my feelings you should be concerned with, madam.'

Ben's eyes returned to the road, missing the frown on Verity's face at the inevitable 'attractive'. She was developing an irrational dislike for the word, which in her opinion could have been applied to the countryside around them just as well. She wanted him to say something less lukewarm, like alluring, sexy even. He noticed her silence, but made no comment, eventually turning the car on to the grass verge when the road widened slightly. He undid his seatbelt and turned to her.

'What is it, Verity?' His eyes searched her face.

She looked at him in surprise. 'Nothing. Why have we stopped, I thought we were late.'

116

'We are. But something's wrong, and I'd like to put it right.'

Verity avoided his eyes. 'Even sensible girls like me get nervous on occasion, Ben.'

He looked sceptical and touched her lip with his forefinger. 'Do you mean nerves, or cold feet? If you've changed your mind, perhaps now would be the time to tell me, before we involve my parents.'

Verity was silent, a cold feeling of dismay in the pit of her stomach.

'Well?' he prompted. 'Have you?'

'No—not exactly.'

'What the hell does that mean? Look at me Verity!' Ben jerked her face round to his, his eyes boring into hers. She stared back at him mutinously, her chin lifting.

'Nothing. I meant I can't help feeling my original reservations, that's all.'

Ben looked at her for a long time, his face grim, until Verity grew restive and pushed away his hand, turning her head away.

'What I should have done last night,' he said at last, his voice almost reflective, 'was finish what I started. I should have gone on making love to you until you had no doubts left about anything. Who knows? The thought of our marriage might have become a cast-iron certainty in your mind—the workings of which I don't pretend to understand.' He gave a mirthless laugh. 'You might have felt it was necessary to be made an honest woman and all that.'

Verity looked at him with distaste, her eyes bright and cold.

'Because you'd had your evil way with me? You're a decade or two behind the times. You may be the squire, but I'm hardly the village maiden. This is the age of equal rights—in all departments.' She added the last deliberately, taking an obscure pleasure in the sudden rigidity of Ben's face.

'I see,' he said distantly, and looked at his watch.

'Well? Speak now, Miss Marsh. Which way shall we go. Forward or back?'

It was plain he meant more than just the evening ahead. Their entire relationship was teetering, hanging on what she said next. Verity felt stricken. The silly disagreement was her fault entirely, and unless she wanted to whistle her marriage down the wind she would have to do something about it, fast. It was unrealistic to want the moon, when everything any sane woman could want was already here, in the palm of her tightly clenched hand. She looked at Ben, who sat staring through the windscreen, his big body tense, the heat from his skin reaching hers across the small space that separated them.

'I'm sorry, Ben,' she said quietly. 'I'm not normally temperamental. If you still want me to I'll be happy to dine with your parents.'

He let out a deep breath and turned to unfasten her seatbelt.

'I'm beginning to think this is the only way to keep you convinced,' he said unevenly, and kissed her with a vehemence that gave expression to his relief. He drew back, an intense light in his eyes as he looked into hers. 'We're two responsible adults, Verity, old enough to know our own minds. For me that's what matters. Even if my parents disapproved it still wouldn't matter. You are exactly what I want in a wife. How often do I have to keep saying it?'

Verity smiled crookedly, pushing him gently away. 'You don't any more. I'm sorry, I was just being tiresome. Let's go.'

Ben looked at her a moment longer, then drove off without a word, his brows still drawn together. Truce was declared, decided Verity uneasily, but it was a fragile one.

When they reached Temple Priors Sir Hugh and Lady Dysart were standing in the open doorway to greet them.

'My dear, welcome!' Isabel Dysart came forward with

hands outstretched and kissed Verity's cheek warmly.
'We are so very pleased to see you again.'

Sir Hugh added his own welcome, his shrewd eyes,
black like Ben's, taking note of Verity's high colour and
his son's lack of conversation as they all crossed the
cool, dim hall.

'Drinks on the terrace outside,' said Lady Dysart. 'It
seemed a pity to waste such a lovely evening—one can't
help feeling this weather must surely break at any
moment, so I tend to spend as much time as possible
out of doors.'

'So do I, out of working hours,' said Verity.

'How do you like to spend your leisure-time?' asked
Sir Hugh.

'When the weather's good just sunbathing,' she
confessed, 'but I play tennis quite a bit, and in between
wage a constant battle with the garden.'

'Say no more,' he laughed. 'Isabel here would spend
her entire life on her hands and knees grubbing about in
the earth if given the choice.'

Verity could feel Ben's eyes on her as she sat down in
a wicker chair, conscious of his amusement as she was
immediately plunged into the world of horticulture, any
constraint she might have felt dispelled at once by Lady
Dysart's enthusiasm. Her gradual unwinding was
helped on enormously by the consumption of two
lethally dry Martinis in quick succession. She emerged
from an account of her mother's special remedy against
greenfly to notice Ben waving away the Martini pitcher
when his father offered him a refill.

'Driving, Dad.'

Lady Dysart frowned. 'It's pity you have to drive
Verity back. After all, we all know why we're here—to
welcome Verity into the family. I don't know why we're
avoiding the subject!'

'Mother's passion for gardening has side effects,' Ben
told Verity, straight-faced. 'She believes in calling a
spade a spade.'

Lady Dysart ignored him, turning to Verity with a

smile. 'Martha has cooked rather a special meal, Hugh has dug out some Burgundy he's been keeping for a special occasion, not to mention the obligatory champagne, so you must stay the night, then Ben can drink what he likes.'

Verity flashed a look of enquiry at Ben, who shrugged slightly, leaving the decision to her. She waved a hand at her silk dress.

'If Ben doesn't mind getting up early to get me back home to change in the morning, why yes, that's a lovely idea. Thank you.' She looked up deliberately at Ben. 'It really would be a pity if you couldn't celebrate our engagement wholeheartedly, wouldn't it darling?'

Ben's eyes flickered for an instant, then he rose to his feet and bent down to kiss her, her shoulders cupped in his hard hands as his mouth lingered on hers. Verity's cheeks were scarlet when he released her, to the approval of his smiling parents, who plainly enjoyed the little demonstration very much.

'That's more like it, Ben,' said his father, winking.

'Frankly I sensed a bit of a chill in the air when you arrived,' said Lady Dysart candidly.

'There was,' said Ben. He pulled his chair closer to Verity's and took her hand in his. 'We had a slight argument on the way, which is why we're late.'

'My fault entirely,' said Verity. 'I hope it hasn't held up the meal.' The warmth of the hard hand holding hers was generating a warmth through her entire body quite different from the excitement of the night before, a glow of well-being replacing the uncertainty that had dogged her since Ben's proposal. She smiled her apology at Lady Dysart, who shook her head vigorously.

'The soup is chilled and Martha is only now concocting the sauce to go with the meat, so nothing's spoiled, Verity.' She glanced from one to the other with undisguised curiosity in her pretty blue eyes. 'Are we allowed to ask why you disagreed?'

'A matter of snobbery, Mother,' said Ben, 'the

inverted variety.' Verity shot a kindling look at him but he went on blandly, 'Verity is obsessed with the notion that you two would prefer a more aristocratic daughter-in-law.'

Verity tried to withdraw her hand, but Ben's fingers tightened.

'I see.' Lady Dysart shook her head at her son. 'And of course you told her it didn't matter a hang what we thought, as you were the one she was marrying.'

Ben's smile flashed in a gleaming grin. 'Bang on target, Mother.'

'Idiot,' said his father amiably, and topped up Verity's drink. 'No wonder the girl looked a bit tense when she arrived.' He patted her cheek. 'All right now though, eh?'

'Perfectly, thank you.' Verity smiled serenely and raised her glass to him.

'Mind you, I can appreciate how you felt,' Lady Dysart said matter-of-factly. 'Old Lady Dysart, Hugh's mother, thought he could have done a lot better than me, I assure you, but all that sort of thing is frightfully out of date these days.' She gave Verity a knowing little smile. 'Ben says you spent the weekend with your mother—I'm sure she disagreed with you.'

Verity laughed. 'Yes. She did. Her view was that our family is rather longer on respectability than lineage, but otherwise her daughter was good enough for anybody.'

'Hear, hear,' said Sir Hugh genially.

'A lady of good sense,' said Ben. 'I shall ask her formal consent as soon as possible—I'd like to meet her.'

The sound of a gong interrupted them, and Lady Dysart shepherded them off to the dining-room at the double, confiding that Martha was a dear soul, but inclined to turn belligerent if her meals were kept hanging about.

With good reason, as Verity found out with her first spoonful of asparagus soup, which was as good to look at as to taste, with its small island of parsley-speckled cream floating in each gold-rimmed white bowl. Now that the air had been cleared so successfully she approached dinner with her normal healthy appetite, finishing off the pale green soup to await the main course with anticipation as Martha carried the dishes in. Sir Hugh noted her enthusiasm warmly.

'Can't stand a female who pecks at her food,' he announced and passed a superb oyster sauce for Verity to spoon over her rump steak. 'I like to see a woman enjoy her food.'

'Then Verity's your girl,' Ben told him.

'Very sensible.' His mother pressed Verity to mushrooms en brochette and soufflé potatoes. 'If you work hard and take a lot of exercise, you need good food. Salad, dear?'

Verity accepted everything offered her, including the quite magnificent wine that Sir Hugh poured into the crystal goblet in front of her. Under the mellowing effect of the delicious food and the feeling of celebration in the air she became quite expansive about her work and the property market in general, even asking Sir Hugh questions about the Temple Priors estate, which seemed to please him a great deal. After a pudding of pears poached in Chablis, followed by some ripe Stilton, they drank coffee and brandy in the drawing-room, lingering for only a short time before Ben sprang to his feet, holding out his hand to Verity.

'We'll be back for the champagne later, Mother. I'd like Verity to have a look at Tern Cottage—see what she wants in the way of furniture.'

'Yes, of course. Thank goodness that tiresome Layton girl has moved. Having her so near at hand was somewhat embarrassing,' said his mother with candour.

'Her name's Middleton now, Mother.' Ben glanced at Verity slyly. 'And be careful—Verity was at school with Gussie, you know.'

'Sorry, dear,' said Lady Dysart, unperturbed. 'You'll

get used to me—I'm inclined to put my foot in it now and then.'

Verity was quite unconcerned. 'That was a long time ago, Lady Dysart. Gussie just happened to be my room-mate in school—we were never really close.' She smiled at Ben sweetly. 'But it meant I did learn rather a lot about Ben before I ever actually met him.'

Sir Hugh coughed loudly as he lit a cigar. 'Nothing very good, I'll be bound. Silly little thing she was at one time.'

'No more silly than I was,' said Ben, and took Verity's arm. 'Come on, let's go for a little drive.'

'Oh, but I thought——'

'I haven't had all that much to drink, and in any case I'll use the Landrover and keep to the farm track on our land. It runs down to the water-meadows on this side of the river. We can reach the cottage on foot from there.'

Verity asked the Dysarts to pass on her compliments to Martha on the splendid dinner and went with Ben. The mention of Gussie had failed to disturb her in the slightest she found, as she was hoisted into the front seat of the Landrover by Ben's powerful arms. He looked in doubt at the fragile heels of her kid sandals and touched a finger to her bare instep.

'Will you be able to walk in those?'

She was unconcerned. 'If not I'll go barefoot.'

'Or I can carry you.' His fingers encircled her ankle.

'I'm no featherweight!'

'I've carried heavier packs than you before now.' He smiled and released her ankle slowly before getting in to drive off.

Verity seemed filled with some new vitality, the blood throbbing along her veins with a new awareness of life as the vehicle went carefully along the bumpy track between fields bleached silver in the moonlight. The moon appeared brighter, the stars more luminous, the scent of the grass more aromatic than ever before as they reached the watermeadows. And there, across the river on its rise, its back towards them, stood the cottage.

Verity gazed at it like a pilgrim in sight of Mecca. The plaster walls glimmered white between weathered timbers, the steep, pointed gables casting black angular shadows in the moonlight; a dream house, ephemeral and unreal. She was hardly aware of Ben as she slid off her sandals and took his hand to step down, heedless of uneven hummocky ground beneath her feet, or grass that brushed against her bare legs as he led her towards a narrow, flimsy footbridge, half hidden by protective willows a little way upstream from the house.

'I didn't know there was another bridge at the back of the house!' She broke away from him and danced across, throwing a glittering look at Ben over her shoulder.

'Be carefuly, Verity—you could get splinters in your feet,' he warned.

She shook her hair back, laughing.

'Nothing so mundane as splinters, Ben—not tonight. It's a magic night. Can't you feel it in the air?' She reached the other side and pirouetted round, her arms flung wide, the pleats of her heavy silk dress furling round her. 'See, Ben? I'm not sensible and efficient and capable tonight. I feel reckless, fey—too much wine perhaps, or possibly I'm moonstruck.' She whirled like a dervish, collapsing laughing against him as he caught her in his arms.

'You'll make yourself dizzy,' he muttered, holding her close. Verity leaned back against his arms, her eyes dancing.

'Only tonight, Ben. Tomorrow I'll be sober. That's a song, isn't it? "For tonight I'll merry, merry be, For tonight I'll merry, merry be". . . .'

'Here,' he said, laughing, and pulled her after him up the steep path. 'Come and see the house. Tell me how you want it.'

Verity was breathless when he let her go to unlock the kitchen door, then astonished as he turned on the lights. The room was empty. All the chrome and white space-age gadgetry had gone, leaving the walls bare in all their original glory. Verity rounded on Ben in amazement.

'What happened to all the cupboards and things?'

'I had them taken out,' he said, grinning. 'All that white and red and glitter looked wrong in here. I was sure you'd prefer something different.'

She gave him a spontaneous kiss on the cheek for the first time.

'Clever man, I would, I would.' She circled the room on her bare feet, her eyes shining as she furnished it in imagination. 'Oak cupboards, Ben? With cream and brown rippled tops and the floor the same to counteract the darkness of the wood. Hobs let in here—oven here—double sinks and drainers, overhead cupboards here, yellow curtains, a proper table and ladder-back chairs.' She met Ben's smile guiltily. 'Am I being over-extravagant?'

He shook his head, his eyes indulgent on her flushed face. 'Not so far—come and look at the rest of it.'

The house was empty. Polished black floors reflected white walls and rough-hewn black beams in silence as Verity wandered everywhere at leisure. Nothing remained to remind her of the former tenants. Stripped of its pink velvet and white fur the parlour waited proudly for furnishings more fitting for its age and dignity.

'I was a fool,' said Ben suddenly, his voice echoing.

Verity paused half-way up the stairs, her face mischievous as she looked down at him. 'In which particular instance?' she asked sweetly.

He gave her a sharp tap on her behind, and propelled her up to the landing at speed, standing with her at the top to look down into the hall below.

'I now realise that I should have brought you here first and then asked you to marry me,' he explained, a wry twist to his mouth. 'I needn't have had last weekend to endure. You'd have said yes at once, without putting me through all that uncertainty.'

'Was it so bad?' she asked curiously, wishing that his face were more expressive.

'Yes,' he said briefly. 'It was. Do you want to see the bedrooms?'

'Are they empty?' asked Verity, wandering into the master bedroom to find it was not. She stopped short at the sight of the made-up bed that was the only item of furniture.

'I sleep here for the time being.' Ben leaned in the doorway, arms folded, the light of mockery in his eyes very pronounced for once. 'I don't keep it for private orgies, I merely dislike the idea of the place empty and vulnerable.'

'Oh.' Verity looked at him in silence. Ben looked back steadily, then put out a hand and switched off the light. Faint moonlight lit the room, transforming it to an other-worldly place of light and shadow, turning Verity's eyes to pools of darkness as she stood perfectly still, rooted to the floor, the polished boards cool against the soles of her feet as Ben left the doorway and moved towards her slowly.

'Time we went home,' he said.

Verity nodded wordlessly and stayed where she was.

'You'll have cold feet,' he added.

'Warm them, then,' she whispered and melted into the arms he held out to her, her mouth meeting his hungrily as their bodies flowed together, eager for contact. Verity stirred reluctantly. 'My dress will crease—your parents——'

He laid a finger on her lips then turned her round, sliding down the zip on her dress until she could step out of it. Verity stood quietly in her satin slip, watching Ben hang her dress over the wooden balustrade outside on the landing, waiting for him to come back to her. He lifted her and sat down on the bed with her on his knees, looking at her questioningly for a moment. She said nothing but, satisfied with what he read in her eyes, Ben drew her down to lie full length against him. They were silent, not even kissing, strangely peaceful in the uncurtained room, a ray of moonlight falling across their closely entwined bodies.

For a long, almost unreal interval Ben went on holding Verity close without speaking, until gradually the quality of the silence altered. The posture of his body changed, tensed, and communicated its tension to hers. His arms tightened, and involuntarily she moved closer to him, feeling his breath hot against her cheek as it quickened. Gently one of his hands began to stroke her shining hair, moving down to her shoulders and her yielding waist, then down her spine, lower and lower, retreating as he felt her stiffen slightly. The hand retraced its path upwards until it reached her chin and brought her mouth to his, and he made a muffled sound deep in his throat as she returned his kiss with an ardour that left him shaken.

'Verity.' His face was stern as he held her away from him. 'I know it's hard to believe, but when I took off your dress I never intended——'

'I know.' Verity laid a finger dreamily on his lips. He took it between his teeth and bit gently, his chest rising and falling unevenly against hers, his heart hammering in a way that aroused and excited her. Voluptuously she curled closer against him, only half aware of her actions, the moonlight, the wine, the walk barefoot in the moonlight all components of the enchantment that held them fast in a fragile, sensuous bubble.

'I want you,' he said abruptly.

'I know.'

'You should be trying to escape.'

'Why? I don't want to.'

'Verity——'

'Sh, Ben,' her dreamy sigh ended against his mouth as he gave up, victim of the same inevitability affecting the girl in his arms. Swiftly and silently he stripped off his clothes, then, with infinite care, the remainder of hers before taking her in his arms. Neither was proof against the effect of body touching body, bare skin on bare skin. Mere physical contact was the ignition to the fire that enveloped them both simultaneously as each caressed the other in an ecstatic harmony of lips and hands and bodies ruled by a mutual, irresistible desire to merge and possess. It was over quite quickly, too fierce a heat to burn for very long without consuming them completely. Afterwards they lay in stunned silence, still locked together, unwilling to break apart. At last Verity stirred.

'We should go back,' she whispered.

'Is that all you have to say?' Ben held her fast, refusing to move.

'Ben——' but her protest was half-hearted and he knew it. Nothing more was said as the fire rekindled, to burn steadily for much longer this time before the final conflagration overtook them once more.

'Now we really must go—it's late,' said Verity imperatively, and reluctantly Ben released her, getting to his feet to dress himself with speed while she did the same. They stole back down the stairs, pausing to laugh at their own stealth as they switched off lights and locked up. Heedless of her bare feet in her moon-mad euphoria on the way up to the cottage, Verity found she was conscious of every bump and stone on the way back, but refused to let Ben carry her on the grounds of speed.

'We must be very late,' she said anxiously, searching for her sandals when they reached the Landrover.

Ben glanced at his watch as he drove off. 'Not that much. We left the house exactly one hour and ten minutes ago, so we haven't been overlong. Besides, they know exactly where we are.'

But not what we've been doing, Verity thought silently, still profoundly shaken by the experience. 'It seems longer than that.' Her eyes turned to meet Ben's, her stomach muscles contracting at the look he gave her before concentrating on the uneven track.

'There was no preconceived plan about what happened back there, Verity,' he said huskily. 'I didn't take you to the cottage with the intention of seducing you.'

'You didn't seduce me,' said Verity with justice. 'We were just overtaken by circumstances, wouldn't you say?'

Ben stopped the vehicle near the ruined stables and jumped out. He lifted Verity out, holding her against his chest, her feet clear of the ground.

'I never dreamed——' he began, his lips almost touching hers.

'Neither did I.' Verity's lids dropped before the gleam of possession in his eyes, her face hot. Ben kissed her at length, finally letting her go only when an exaggeratedly loud cough interrupted them as the figure of Sir Hugh strolled out of the shadows.

'If you could just put her down for a while Ben,' he said dryly. ' I could open the champagne and propose a toast. Your mother was beginning to wonder where you were.'

'Coming, Dad.' Ben put an arm round Verity's waist as the three of them returned to the house by way of the terrace to join Lady Dysart in the drawing-room. She took off her reading-glasses and put down her book, looking at Ben and Verity in amusement.

'I was just about to have a cup of tea and forget about the champagne. Come and sit beside me, Verity, and tell me how you've decided to furnish while Hugh wrestles with the champagne cork.'

Verity sat down on the brocade settee feeling completely at peace with the world, entirely free from the doubts and uncertainties of recent weeks, not even unduly embarrassed because her face was now bare of make-up and her hair frankly untidy. She accepted a glass of champagne with a radiant smile, still inwardly a little dazed from her first encounter with sexual fulfilment. Ben slid down beside her, a possessive arm along her shoulders as they drank a toast to their own future.

'How soon will the wedding be?' asked Lady Dysart with interest.

Ben glanced down at Verity.

'Six weeks? Or I could get a special licence——'

'I say, steady on son,' said his father, chuckling. 'We've been at you for years to take the plunge and now you want to rush off and tie the knot in five minutes.'

Ben grinned. 'Can you blame me?'

His mother leaned across and patted his hand.

'No darling, not in the least, but let Verity have her say. She's the bride and the choice is her privilege.'

The bride. The word brought Verity up short, starting up a whole new train of thought. Ben might expect her to give up her job, and there was her house and Jenny and Henrietta to consider.

Ben gave her a nudge.

'Wake up, beautiful dreamer—give us your view on the subject!'

'I can't decide just like that,' she said firmly. 'Definitely no special licence anyway, and even six weeks is pushing it a bit. The whole idea is new to me, after all—marriage was never part of my calculations up to now.'

'That's right; don't let him bully you,' approved Lady Dysart, then hesitated. 'I'm trying to be tactful——'

'Which is an effort,' teased her son.

'Really Ben! What I'm trying to say is that when you do decide on the date I hope Verity's mother would be kind enough to allow us to hold the reception here?' Lady Dysart looked questioningly at Verity, who put out a hand warmly and touched the other woman's in reassurance.

'I'm quite sure she would. We'll get it all settled as soon as possible. In fact, if you'd like us to be married in the church here I'm quite happy about that too.'

The gratitude on the older Dysarts' faces was reward enough, and Sir Hugh insisted on broaching another bottle while Ben kissed Verity swiftly, his quiet thanks intensifying the glow in her eyes.

It was very late when Sir Hugh and Lady Dysart

finally went to bed with fond goodnights, and directions to Ben on where Verity was to sleep. There was silence in the big, graceful room after they left as Ben and Verity remained where they were on the long sofa.

'Are you happy Verity?' he asked at last.

She turned thoughtful eyes up to his. 'Very happy. Quite apart from the champagne and the moonlight and—and all the other events of this quite extraordinary evening, I have never been so happy in my whole life.'

Ben gripped her hand hard. 'You are a very unusual lady, Verity. Haven't you felt that something was missing this evening, despite the action-packed programme?'

Verity's heart stood still, then resumed beating heavily. This, then, was the moment her entire being had longed for. Through all the fierce intensity of their lovemaking neither of them had spoken, all their energies concentrated into the physical act. No word of love had been uttered—no sound at all until that final groan of triumph wrung from Ben as they reached the climax together. She sat, expectant and tense, willing him to say he loved her.

'Well?' he prompted.

'I'm not quite sure what you mean,' she said quietly, her eyes on her hands.

'In just three little words, bride-to-be, an engagement ring!'

Tossed to the heights then plunged to the depths in the space of one sentence, Verity's mental equilibrium suffered badly. She stood up, eluding the hands that tried to restrain her. She smiled brightly down into Ben's questioning face, rigidly controlling her disappointment.

'I never gave it a thought.' Which was the complete truth. 'I'm not really a jewellery person, Ben. Just the wedding ring will do.'

He got slowly to his feet, a look of disbelief on his dark features as he thrust a hand through his hair in a gesture which was becoming familiar to Verity.

'A pearl among women! Though your attitude has rather a dampening effect on my romantic intentions.' With a crooked smile he reached into the pocket of his white linen shirt and took out a twist of tissue-paper, holding it out to her. 'I should have given you this down at the cottage, but what happened there drove everything out of my head.'

Verity stood looking at the paper in his hand in silence until he moved nearer and unwrapped the ring it contained, holding it out on his palm. Numbly she saw that it was beautiful, a cluster of rubies and diamonds in an antique clawed setting, the gold band wide and heavy. It was obviously old and a little massive for some tastes, but when Ben slid it on her finger it looked very much at home on Verity's capable, long-fingered hand.

'My grandmother left it to me with some other pieces,' he said and kissed her hand, looking up at her from beneath questioning black brows. 'I thought you would like it better than a modern ring, but it's for you to choose.'

'It's lovely.' Verity smiled at him, something of her equanimity restored. 'Exactly to my taste. Thank you.'

'Does it fit?'

'A little loose, but not enough to alter it.' Verity admired the flash of the stones and waved her hand about to display them, hoping this was standard procedure for the newly-engaged, but very much aware of the frown on Ben's face as he watched her.

'What is it Verity?'

'Nothing.' She turned wide, serene eyes on him. 'What could be the matter on a night like this?'

'Some of your candlepower has dimmed.' He put an arm round her and drew her close, holding up her face with peremptory fingers to look into her eyes. 'Are you regretting what happened between us tonight?'

On this point, at least, Verity could be completely honest.

'How could I? You were no more responsible than I.

What happened—just *happened*. I had no idea, I admit, that one was overtaken by such an irresistible force.'

Ben's teeth gleamèd white for an instant. 'One seldom is. We experienced something quite rare, take my word for it.'

Verity smiled ruefully. 'You disappoint me. I assumed it would always be like that.'

'If it's within my power to make it so, believe me it will!' He kissed her, holding her close against him, until there were unmistakable signs that if not damped down sharply their mutual bonfire was likely to get out of hand yet again. 'You see?' He shook her slightly, his voice unsteady. 'We have something very special, you and I, Verity. More than most. Don't keep me waiting too long.'

For hours after Ben left her at the door of the pretty room made ready for her, Verity lay in the comfortable bed, wide-eyed and sleepless, twisting the heavy ring on her finger, his words echoing in her mind. 'More than most' and 'something special' chased round and round in her head. He was right, of course, and she would just have to be satisfied. Tonight had proved their physical compatability beyond all doubt, that was obvious. She turned on her stomach and buried her head in the pillows at the mere memory of her utter abandon, so complete that she had barely registered the fleeting pang as he took her for the first time. His manners were good, she granted him that, having the good grace to refrain from asking why, at her advanced age, she had never gone this far before. Perhaps he hadn't noticed. The truth would have been a bit embarrassing. How could she have explained that all her adult life she had been waiting for just that very combination of mental and physical cataclysm to sweep her off her feet as it had done tonight. But overwhelming as it was, it still wasn't enough. She wanted Ben head over heels in love with her as well.

Ben was fond of her, respected her, and now it was proved beyond all doubt that he wanted her body as much as he needed her capabilities. Verity turned on her side and settled herself determinedly to sleep, vowing fiercely that somehow she would *make* him fall in love with her. One day he'd be on his knees—at this her natural good sense reasserted itself and she smiled in the darkness. It was impossible to imagine Ben on his knees, somehow, and if he were she rather fancied she wouldn't care for him in supplicating mood anyway. Ben would demand, not beg, and one day, as sure as God made little apples, he'd demand her love in return for his own.

CHAPTER EIGHT

'A FINE romance, with no kisses' was the tune echoing in Verity's head for the next few weeks as she lived her life in a frenetic, unending round of hard work and wedding arrangements which left little time, or inclination, for much dalliance of any kind between herself and Ben. The property-market was having a final energy-consuming fling before dying down for the winter, and the eventual wedding date was set for the end of October, when Verity felt she could leave Lockhart & Welch with a clear conscience and no feeling of desertion.

'I'd never have let Ben Dysart within a mile of you if I'd thought he'd spirit you away,' grumbled John Randall good-naturedly. 'Can't see why you have to leave. Most women work after marriage these days.'

'I'm no exception,' said Verity tartly. 'Ben needs a helping hand with the estate and I'm going to supply it.'

'Sounds very businesslike, the whole thing,' he said morosely. 'Ben might just as well have offered you a job instead of proposing, it seems to me.'

'Thanks.' Verity gave him a fulminating look as she opened his office door to leave. 'It just so happens he wants a wife as well.'

'Lucky chap to get two for the price of one!' John's eyes twinkled, but Verity's sense of humour had become a sensitive plant of late.

'You do wonders for my ego, Mr Randall,' she snapped, and flounced out, but he called her back.

'Sorry, sweetheart,' he said sincerely. 'Did I touch an exposed nerve?'

Verity relaxed and smiled apologetically. 'Think nothing of it. I have it on the best authority that all bridal nerves are entitled to expose themselves. Sounds faintly rude—I'd better be off.'

Verity and Ben saw each other at irregular intervals, occasionally at the cottage, but never at night, and rarely alone, as the place was usually alive with workmen fitting the kitchen, or painting.

In fact, the odd mixture of restraint and camaraderie Ben showed towards Verity brought her to the point of despair at times, and yet at others glad of the breathing space that allowed them to get to know each other better. Whereas before there had been uncertainty and sexual tension in their relationship, now they had time to learn more about each other, tastes, backgrounds, feelings and opinions, a surprising amount of which they had in common, as Ben had insisted from the first.

Their first trip together had been to Birkenhead to meet her mother and Ian. This was a great success, as both Hannah and Ian Craig liked Ben Dysart on sight, a feeling which was mutual, to Verity's relief, as her mother was sometimes a little outspoken for some people's tastes. Ben enjoyed Hannah's directness, responding in like manner, not permitting her to bully him into eating the sweet things she most enjoyed cooking. It was in an effort to deflect his wife's persistence that Ian caused the only apprehensive moment Verity experienced the entire weekend. They had been sitting over dinner on the first evening, Ben resolutely eating his usual cheese, in spite of Hannah's blandishments.

'Such a shame,' she said regretfully, 'when you obviously don't need to watch your weight.' She passed an enormous plateful of blackberry pie smothered in cream to her husband. 'Ian here eats cakes, pudding, anything you care to name and never puts on an ounce. He has some defence-mechanism against calories— worth a fortune if he could market it.'

'I think they call it hard work,' said Ian mildly and turned to Ben with the obvious intention of changing the subject. 'I gather you've recently returned to civilian life from the Royal Marines—it must be quite a re-adjustment.'

Verity held her breath. Ben never volunteered much about his life in the Marines, but to her surprise began to talk quite naturally about it, his audience deeply interested about his training at Lympstone and Dartmouth.

'The life of an officer isn't quite all cakes and ale,' he said with a grin. 'At Lympstone one was obliged to complete the thirty-mile speed march in seven hours to the recruits' eight, which was a shade testing.'

Ian shuddered. 'Killing sounds a more appropriate description!'

'There are compensations, of course. Every marine must become a qualified skier, and I've always enjoyed that type of thing.'

Verity suddenly remembered a broad-shouldered outline advancing towards her in the unlit cottage, moonlight playing on the long, flat muscles she now realised were the characteristic of the accomplished skier. Heat ran through her and her mouth went dry at the memory of what had followed the first contact of that superb body against her own. She started violently as she realised her mother was speaking to her, colouring as three pairs of eyes looked at her in amusement.

'Verity, I was asking you to fetch the coffee—you were miles away,' said Hannah.

'Sorry!' Guiltily Verity jumped up, glad to escape, taking her time before returning, by which time the conversation had turned to other matters.

The rest of their stay passed pleasantly, and they were on the way home on the Sunday when Ben remarked idly, 'What were you thinking about on Friday evening when I was talking about my training?'

'I can't remember,' lied Verity.

'Yes you can. You went bright red—an endearing habit of yours—when your mother called your name for the third time. Come on, out with it.'

'It was nothing, really,' said Verity irritably. 'Merely that when you mentioned being a qualified skier I realised how you came by your muscles.'

'And you thought of the time in the cottage?'

'Yes.'

'I see. And was the memory pleasant?'

She shot him a suspicious glance, but his profile was unreadable as usual.

'Not unpleasant, certainly,' she said.

'Oh Verity, how grudging!' Ben gave her a wicked, sidelong grin that evoked an unwilling response, which changed to a chuckle.

'Straight on top of Mother's duck and orange sauce the memory had rather an alarming effect!'

'I hope you're not equating my lovemaking with indigestion!' He sounded injured.

Verity smiled demurely, staring straight ahead. 'No, I wouldn't do that,' privately wishing she could, as there were remedies for indigestion, whereas the feeling that gripped her at Ben's merest touch seemed likely to be incurable.

'Personally I don't think further moonlit visits to the cottage very advisable, while we're on the subject,' went on Ben casually.

Verity knew he was right, but felt disproportionately annoyed that the suggestion had come from Ben rather than herself.

'No,' she said coolly. 'It might be a good idea to cut out that sort of thing altogether until we're married.'

Ben turned a wary eye on her averted face. 'Entirely? Not even a goodnight kiss?'

'I meant it might be best if we avoided long periods alone anywhere,' she said grinning, her sense of humour returning. 'I mean, I know you want a family, but from my point of view I'd just as soon the first member appeared after a respectable interval, don't you agree?'

Ben's face lost its impassivity. 'My God!' He took a hand off the wheel and ran it through his hair. 'Do you mean——?'

'Don't panic,' she said kindly. 'Let's just say this time we were lucky—next time might be less—or more—opportune. Whichever way you like to think of it.'

He let out a long breath. 'You're taking it very calmly.'

'I do my best,' she said smugly. 'Are you coming in when we get back?'

'Isn't that a rash invitation under the circumstances?'

'Not really. Now you're alive to the risk I'm sure you'll proceed accordingly.' Verity stole a look at him. 'I suppose you've never had to think about it before, in this age of enlightenment.' Her eyes narrowed. 'Though I seem to remember Gussie——'

'Can we leave Gussie out of it,' he snapped. 'I find schoolgirl reminiscences distasteful in the extreme under the circumstances.'

Deeply offended Verity maintained a distant silence for the remainder of the journey, glad when they arrived. There was no lightening of Ben's black mood as he took her suitcase from the car into the house, a mere brief goodbye his only word at parting, with no mention of their next meeting before he drove off. It was a welcome relief to find both her young tenants were in, happy to ply her with tea and put forward a new proposal about the future.

'The thing is, Verity, will you want to put the house up for sale?' asked Jenny.

Verity disliked the idea intensely. The thought of her retreat completely cut off gave her a defenceless feeling that accentuated the depression she was feeling at Ben's cold departure.

'No,' she said with decision. 'I won't. Though I don't quite see what I'm going to do with it.'

'Well that's just it,' said Henrietta eagerly. 'I'm pretty sure I have the chance to come back again next season, and I know one or two girls in the company who'd jump at the chance of Jenny's room.'

'You mean leave the ground floor empty?'

'No,' said Jenny, her eyes shining. 'Richard and I

haven't found anywhere we like that we can afford, so I thought perhaps you'd let the ground floor to us. Our wedding's only a week before yours, so——'

'Great! Wonderful!' Verity smiled in relief. 'I can't think why I didn't suggest it myself.'

'Perhaps our sensible landlady has had her head just slightly in the clouds lately,' suggested Henrietta slyly. 'And who could blame you!'

'Yes, things have been a bit hectic,' agreed Verity and stretched wearily. 'Never mind, there's plenty of time yet before the wedding.'

She went to bed early for once, with a long glass of lemonade spiked with Cinzano beside her as she tried to concentrate on a very complicated John Le Carré novel, when the phone rang beside her bed.

'I'm sorry,' said Ben's voice without preliminary. There was a pause. 'Verity?'

'Yes.' She felt tongue-tied, gauche, with nothing to say.

'Are you still angry with me?'

'No. Anyway, I thought you were the one in a temper,' she pointed out.

'I was. But I'm not now. Where are you?'

'In bed.'

'I'd rather you didn't mention bed.' His voice roughened.

'You asked.'

'I know. But it conjures up immediate visions of the last time I saw you lying on a bed, this bed, where I am right now.'

Verity took a deep breath. 'You're in bed early.'

'There was nothing else to do. I was bored. I miss you. So I came down here with some Scotch and the Sunday papers.' The roughness was gone, replaced by a caressing note that lifted the hairs on Verity's neck. She gave a breathless laugh.

'I've got Cinzano and a John Le Carré.'

'Why did we set the wedding so far away!'

'It was the date that suited everyone.'

'It damn' well doesn't suit me,' he growled. 'I want you here with me tonight, right this minute . . .' and for some time he made verbal love to her down the line, leaving her flushed and restless for the entire night.

The wait might have seemed long in some ways, but Verity hardly found it long enough in others. Furnishings at the cottage had been left to a minimum, both of them in agreement that a period actually living there would give them more idea of what they wanted, and in the meantime only the kitchen and the bedroom were actually complete in every detail—getting the priorities right, as Ben termed it. Hannah and Ian were contributing a beautiful Shiraz carpet for the drawing-room as their gift, the Dysarts some exquisite silver and china. In addition to this Isabel Dysart pressed Verity to choose anything from Temple Priors she wanted in the way of furniture as a stop-gap, and with gratitude Verity accepted a matching chair and sofa, both a little shabby, but still elegant, also a cabinet and a small inlaid table. Ben's stereo equipment would fill up some space, and he bought a television for both drawing-room and bedroom.

'Not that I intend to watch too much television in bed,' he informed Verity with a grin, 'but if we want to spend an entire cold Sunday up there now and then it might come in handy.'

'Sounds a bit sinful,' said Verity absently, absorbed in samples of curtain materials to blend with one of the lovely muted shades in the carpet.

'I have great hopes it will be!' He was leaning in the doorway, arms folded as usual, watching her on her knees among snippets of silk and velvet, her hair swinging forward across her face. She stayed still for a moment, then looked up at him with a frown of disapproval at odds with the smile in her eyes.

'I thought we agreed not to think about things like that while we're here.'

'I know.' With a lithe movement he came down on

his knees in front of her. 'But it's bloody difficult. Kiss me. Now!'

Verity obeyed, only to find herself on her back with Ben above her kissing her all over her face and rapidly moving his mouth down her throat, at which point she pushed him away with a superhuman heave, panting as she sat up to smooth back her hair.

'Go away,' she said crossly. 'Find something to do somewhere else.'

Ben jumped up and held out his hand. 'Let's have some coffee in our new kitchen.'

This part of the house was complete, even to some basic provisions in the cupboards, and some everyday pottery. They sat on the new rush-seated chairs at the table near the rear window of the kitchen, overlooking the slope of the back lawn and the screen of willows bending in a graceful frieze along the river bank in the mellow sunset light.

'Oh Ben, it's so beautiful.' Verity gave a sigh of pleasure as she sipped her coffee. 'I can hardly believe it's all true.'

Ben leaned back in his chair, his eyes absent on the garden, an ironic twist to his wide mouth.

'Life's an odd game,' he said meditatively. 'When you consider that my career involved me in various situations of danger, including an actual war, it was far more on the cards that I should have been killed, not poor Nick, who bought it in such an unnecessary, stupid accident at home.'

Verity sat very still, hardly daring to breathe for fear of checking Ben's rare instinct to confide.

'He should have been the soldier,' he went on. 'As a youngster he loved roughing it, climbing, camping and so on—there's quite a bit of his stuff in the outhouse here. I brought it down from the house out of Dad's way; less painful. He still blames himself just for not being here when the accident happened. Illogical, but understandable. Oddly enough I was the one who'd have been quite happy to help with the estate, but when

Nick's asthma grew worse in his teens it became obvious the army was no life for him, so we switched roles. Only I broke with tradition by making it the Royal Marines. As part of a commando brigade I felt I would at least be involved in arctic training and skiing, and be more likely to be sent where the action was.'

Verity watched his swarthy, sombre face with sympathy, her chin propped in her hands as she waited for him to continue. Ben's head turned and he met the compassion in her eyes, the hard, set expression of his own softening as he put out a hand to touch her cheek.

'I don't know what started me on all this,' he said with apology.

'Please go on—no one talks about your brother,' said Verity gently.

'Mother would, at length if we'd let her, but Dad and I find it difficult. Silly really. One can't pretend the entire thing never happened—but God, it was such a bloody awful way to go!' Ben's hand caught hers in a painful grip as he turned away to the window. 'That's what I find so damned hard to forget. If only the stable-lad hadn't nipped down to the village—if only Martha had woken up sooner—and most of all if only some idiot hadn't thrown a cigarette end down in the vicinity. The gates to the main road are close by. It could have been anybody.'

Verity returned the painful grip with helpless sympathy, her throat thickening with unshed tears.

'He wasn't burnt to death,' said Ben harshly. 'That's been some sort of consolation. Help arrived before that stage. But by then the smoke had been too much for him.' His voice cracked on the last words and he got to his feet jerkily, his back turned as he stood staring through the window. She let him be for a while then moved round the table and stood behind him, laying her face silently against his broad back as she slid her arms round his waist and held him close. They stayed like that for a minute or two before he twisted in her grasp and took her in his arms.

'I'm sorry, Verity.' Ben had himself in hand again. 'I had no intention of harrowing you like that.'

'I'm glad,' she said swiftly. 'I hope you'll always talk to me about everything, good and bad. If a marriage is to be a partnership we should try to share everything.'

'A partnership.' There was an odd whimsical look in the eyes that stared down into her candid face. 'Anything you say, wife-to-be. I'm not much given to baring my soul as a rule—you must be a good listener.'

'One of my best features,' smiled Verity.

'I don't think I agree.' His sudden white grin gave her the usual jolt. 'I can think of several others, any one of which I'd be happy to dwell on at length.'

Verity detached herself from his grasp with speed.

'If you're back on that tack let's go! We'll be late for your mother's dinner if we don't hurry up.'

'Heigh-ho!' He strolled after her as she collected up the curtain samples for consultation with Lady Dysart. 'I shall console myself with the thought that soon you'll be cooking dinner for me here with your own fair hands.'

Verity laughed. 'You may not find much consolation in my cooking, I warn you now. Basic is a fair assessment, I'd say.'

'Then you'll have to make it up to me in other ways!' Ben said promptly, chuckling as she hurried ahead of him in exasperation.

The wedding was to be fairly small, Lady Dysart's description rather than Verity's, with only close relatives and friends.

'Though why Ben should feel it necessary to invite Gussie Middleton and her husband I really don't know,' said Lady Dysart in private to Verity.

Neither did Verity, who promptly added Niall Gordon to her own list in a fit of rather immature pique.

'Do you object to Gussie as a wedding guest?' asked Ben as he took her home.

Verity shrugged carelessly. 'Not really. I was invited to *her* wedding.'

'I thought it best, one way and another. Put paid to any gossip there might be,' he said expressionlessly.

'Fine.' Verity smiled up at him sweetly. 'And we've both known her a long time—have you seen her lately?'

'Not since they moved into the Wentworth place. Middleton took her off to Puerto Banus while he had the house decorated for her.'

This was news to Verity, who'd been expecting some kind of visitation from a wrathful Gussie ever since the wedding announcement. Her silence was now explained. When Verity finally did see Gussie a few days later the lady in question was so absorbed in conversation with her companion in a restaurant she failed to spot Verity passing along the pavement outside. So did her companion. He was partly hidden by a curtain, but there was no mistaking the breadth of shoulder in the familiar tweed jacket, nor the tightly curling black hair. It was Ben.

It had been an odd sort of day from the start. Verity should have been in the depths of the Cotswolds, evaluating a sizeable Jacobean house standing in half-an-acre of ground, but the vendor had postponed the appointment to the following week, giving Verity a day in the office with more time for lunch than usual. She had intended to do some shopping, but after seeing Ben with Gussie she changed her mind and bought a sandwich to eat in the park, wandering along the riverbank, and eventually feeding the sandwich to the swans. It was degrading to feel jealous; something new for her in the way of emotions. Verity had never suffered an overpowering desire to claw at someone before in her entire life. She leaned against a tree, indifferent to the cold breeze that blew at her hair and whipped the pleats of her tweed skirt against her legs. Autumn had arrived, the accompanying decrease in temperature in keeping with the chill Verity felt within her.

She wondered bleakly if Ben was making a practice of seeing Gussie. Perhaps they had a regular little arrangement of some kind. Just the previous weekend Verity had met her mother in London to help choose her wedding outfit, staying overnight at a hotel with her, both of them thoroughly enjoying the rare opportunity. Ben had made no mention of his own movements while she was away—perhaps he and Gussie had met at the cottage. Her suspicions were unjust, possibly, but the sight of them together was like acid on her soul, eating away at her all afternoon while she doggedly disposed of as much work as humanly possible as antidote.

Verity went home early and had a leisurely hot bath, complete with book and a glass of wine in an effort to compose herself for Ben's arrival. Nothing would induce her to ask about Gussie, of course, but she felt sure Ben would mention his meeting with her casually, and that would be that.

Ben said nothing at all on the subject. He came round after dinner, accepted a cup of coffee, and launched into an account of his father's plans for enlarging the dairy herd at the home farm, and the probable purchase of a bull. Verity found it hard to concentrate. Every time he paused she waited expectantly, sure that he was about to change the subject to tell her about Gussie.

'What's the matter, Verity?' he asked, when it became fairly obvious his listener's attention was wandering. 'Hard day? It's time you delegated these longer trips to someone else—you won't be there to do them much longer anyway.'

'Haven't been anywhere,' said Verity flatly. 'I was in town all day. The vendor postponed.'

'Then you must have been hard at it at that desk of yours.' Ben patted the sofa beside him invitingly. 'Come here. Even super-efficient ladies like you need cuddling sometimes.'

Verity looked at him steadily. 'I don't think I will, thank you.'

His eyes narrowed. 'I'm not offering a drink or a cup of coffee. I want you to come and relax over here— come on.'

The note of command flicked Verity on the raw. She got up and put the coffee-cups on the tray.

'No. Thanks just the same.' She straightened and looked at him levelly. 'I'm tired, Ben. It might be as well if you went home.'

Ben rose at once, his face set. 'It was hardly worth my coming really, was it?'

'A complete waste of time,' she agreed, 'if all you had in mind was a quick spot of slap and tickle.'

A spark of distaste lit Ben's eyes before they hardened and he made for the door.

'Perhaps you'll ring me tomorrow if you're more in the mood for—my company.'

Verity stayed where she was. 'Fine. I'll do that.'

He stood looking at her for a moment, then turned to go. 'Goodnight then, Verity.'

'Goodnight.'

Verity listened to the car as it roared away, then took the tray to the kitchen, washed and dried the cups and glasses and put them away with meticulous care. She creamed her face and hung up the clothes she took off, then got into bed and began to cry; deep, tearing sobs that sickened and exhausted her, but failed to send her to sleep.

In the cold light of day she viewed the problem dispassionately over a more leisurely breakfast than usual. Verity's appetite, never missing for long, reasserted itself after the privations of the previous day and demanded attention at a fairly early hour, and with her blood sugars restored to normal her usual commonsense took over. Gussie was married to Peter Middleton, and Benedict Dysart was to be joined in marriage with Verity Hannah Marsh at St Augustine's Church, Priorsford, in precisely three weeks' time. These were the facts, and Verity resolved not to give in to petty jealousy again, preparing herself to apologise to Ben for her behaviour the evening before.

Jenny's wedding took place a week before Verity's, both Verity and Henrietta present to wish her well, waving the couple off after the reception in a hail of confetti and old shoes en route for a honeymoon in Marbella.

'Does it feel funny, Verity?' asked Henrietta afterwards. 'Knowing that this time next week you'll also be a married lady?'

'Yes. It does.' They were both drinking coffee in Verity's kitchen in the anti-climactic mood guests usually experience after a wedding. 'Frankly it hasn't sunk in yet. I can't believe that I'm leaving Lockhart and Welch on Wednesday and getting married on Saturday.' She looked around her. 'I'd better do some spring cleaning tomorrow—leave everything spick and span for the happy pair.'

Henrietta looked at her curiously.

'You sound a bit flat, Vee. Pre-wedding nerves and all that?'

'Probably.' Verity stretched and yawned. 'There's been too much to do lately, and now, somehow, there isn't, except wait for the great day, so a few chores won't come amiss.'

'Not seeing Ben tonight?'

'No. He's gone away for the weekend to some sort of reunion. Says he's having his stag night a week early.' Verity spoke lightly but she felt somewhat bereft at the thought of two days without Ben. 'So Saturday night really *is* the loneliest night of the week!'

'Never mind.' Henrietta gave her a saucy grin as she slid off the kitchen table. 'Concentrate on thoughts of *next* Saturday night instead! Must fly, love, time for the performance.'

Thoughts of the following Saturday occupied Verity's mind the entire evening, despite all the scrubbing and polishing. She was glad when the telephone interrupted her, first her mother, who chatted at some length, then one of her old college friends who was coming to the wedding. Each time Verity flew to the phone eagerly, hoping it was Ben, but she was in bed, reading, long after Henrietta had returned from the theatre, before the sudden shrill of the telephone beside her made her jump out of her skin. She picked up the receiver gingerly and said 'Hello' with caution.

'I've caught you at last,' said a familiar voice. Ben's normally crisp tones were slightly blurred and thickened, against a background of convivial uproar that made it difficult to hear him.

'Sounds like a good party,' she remarked.

'Better if you were here. What are you doing?'

'Reading.'

'Where?'

Verity sighed impatiently. 'I'm in bed, Ben, and it's long after midnight. You frightened me out of my wits, you idiot.'

'That's no way to address your betrothed!'

'Very sorry. Go back to your party.'

'Just wanted to wish you goodnight, Verity.'

'Goodnight, Ben.'

She lay back on her pillows, a wry smile on her face. Never any endearments from Ben, not even a casual 'my dear'—not that her own attitude lately had been much encouragement. Since her glimpse of Ben and Gussie together Verity had found it hard to respond to the most restrained of Ben's lovemaking, and lately he had given up trying, treating her with an impersonal friendliness she resented hotly, even though her own behaviour had wrought the change. Sometimes she felt the enchanted moonlit interlude in the cottage had never happened, a mere figment of her imagination. Verity felt bleak as she thought of a marriage where she and Ben remained polite strangers linked together in little more than a business arrangement. There was time to back out even yet, she knew, but Verity quailed at the prospect of cancellation, imagining the feelings of the Dysarts, not to mention her own mother if she

should calmly announce a change of mind. For that was
what it would be, not a change of heart. Ben's feelings
in the matter seemed to have less sympathy from
Verity—she was convinced he would just substitute
someone else in due course if she called the wedding
off.

Verity lunched at Temple Priors next day, and spent
a pleasant afternoon with Ben's parents, chatting over
wedding arrangements and feeling a lot more cheerful
than her black mood of the night before. To her
surprise Ben appeared unexpectedly at tea-time, her
unguarded smile of welcome bringing him swiftly across
the drawing-room to kiss her very thoroughly before
turning to greet his parents.

'Thought you weren't due back until tomorrow,' said
his father.

'I changed my mind,' said Ben without explanation
and sat beside Verity, his arm around her waist.

'No doubt you decided Verity had been left alone
quite long enough,' said his mother approvingly and
handed him a cup of tea.

'Something like that.' Ben's arm tightened and he
dropped a kiss on Verity's hair. 'Can't have her getting
tense with bridal nerves, or whatever it is that girls are
supposed to suffer from.'

'You needn't worry about that,' said Verity, not
entirely candidly. She smiled at him. 'But it's nice to see
you, just the same.'

The constraint of the last week or two was gone, and
Verity sat comfortably in Ben's hold as he gave them a
humorous, watered-down version of his lively evening,
the mood of harmony remaining as he drove her home
after dinner that evening, and sat with her afterwards in
the sitting-room.

'You seemed uptight on the phone last night, Verity,'
he said.

'I'd been indulging in an orgy of housecleaning to
leave the place tidy for Jenny and Richard. Not exactly
my favourite programme for a Saturday night.' Verity

smiled at him ruefully and made no resistance when he
drew her into his arms.

'Perhaps you were missing me,' he suggested softly.

'Perhaps I was.'

'I rang a couple of times earlier in the evening, but
the line was engaged.'

'Did you?' Verity flushed, secretly delighted. 'Mother
rang, then an old college friend who's coming to the
wedding.'

'So now you know why I was so late before I spoke
to you—you cut me off before I could explain.' Ben's
eyes were mocking, and something else that increased
the warmth in Verity's face.

'I'm sorry,' she said penitently.

'Show me how much.'

Verity reached up both hands and brought his face
down to hers. She moved her mouth caressingly against
his, and his arms locked round her in instant reaction as
he returned the kiss with interest. There was no resulting
flash flood of passion, only comfort and reassurance; Ben
made no attempt at further caresses, and after a while
settled her comfortably against his shoulder.

'Something's been troubling you lately, Verity,' he
said bluntly. 'Not second thoughts, I trust?'

Verity hesitated, wondering if she should just come
out with the unvarnished truth—that she had seen Ben
with Gussie, and was jealous as hell. The words stuck in
her throat, and after a pause she shook her head.

'No. At least no more than the usual jitters. It's only
human to wonder how well we'll get on together after
knowing each other such a short time.'

'We shall do very well, so don't trouble yourself on
that score. We are both responsible adults who don't
expect life to be a fairy story. I hope, and expect, there
to be many more nights like that unbelievable time in
the cottage, but we both know that moonlight and
magic are for special occasions and the realities are cold
early mornings and muddy boots, and accounts that
won't balance.' Ben tipped Verity's head back to look

deep in her eyes. 'Am I reassuring you or putting you off altogether?'

Verity searched his dark, intent eyes for any trace of guilt or prevarication, but their black opacity gave nothing away.

'You're absolutely right, of course. At our age it's the realities that count most, not the romance,' she said matter-of-factly, then grinned as he shook her hard.

'I'm not exactly geriatric yet,' he said threateningly. 'There's plenty of life in the old dog yet, I assure you!' And this time his kiss was very much more than merely reassuring, leaving Verity in no doubt that physically, at least, their relationship promised to be everything she could desire.

CHAPTER NINE

THEY were married on one of those still, blue and gold days October provides as a parting gift from autumn.

Verity had resisted all her mother's pleas, refusing to wear a long white dress and traditional veil. 'Not my style, Mother,' she said firmly, and chose a lean, elegant coat-dress in creamy white cashmere with deep satin lapels, the matching sou-wester hat frankly frivolous in contrast, with a nosegay of velvet pansies dropping over one temple from the turned-back satin brim.

As she walked down the aisle on Ian's arm Verity hardly registered the smiling faces turned to watch her progress, all her attention centred on Ben's dark face as she reached his side. Her breath caught as he took her hand and kissed it before they turned to face the Vicar of St Augustine's for the ceremony. Ben's unexpected little greeting gave Verity a glow that remained with her all through the proceedings and the laughing, chaffing bonhomie in the vestry afterwards. Hannah Craig and Isabel Dysart had taken to each other on sight at their first meeting the evening before, to Verity's relief, and it was a very gay assembly who repaired to Temple Priors to partake of a superb buffet luncheon.

After the welter of kisses and congratulations from relatives and friends Gussie and Peter Middleton came along to add their greetings, Gussie's blue eyes narrow and glittering as she kissed the air near Verity's cheek.

'Frightfully well done, darling,' she drawled. 'Peter and I were *so* surprised to hear the news! And tremendously pleased, of course.'

'I say, rather!' agreed Peter, grinning in his usual friendly manner.

'Why thank you, Gussie, you know my mother, and Ben's people of course,' countered Verity with composure, but Gussie wasn't listening, turning away immediately to engage Ben in earnest, whispered conversation, leaving her embarrassed husband to murmur polite inanities. She looked very beautiful, in hyacinth wool crepe, a tiny velvet tricorne on her blonde curls with a long ostrich feather curling on to her flawless cheek. Verity learned little from Ben's face, and turned away abruptly to encounter a sage look from her mother.

'Why Gussie Layton,' said Hannah rather loudly, and detached Gussie adroitly to introduce her to Ian. 'You haven't changed a bit since you were at school with Verity. Do come and meet my husband.'

Verity had no intention of allowing Gussie to spoil her wedding, and put the incident firmly from her mind, enjoying the delicious food and the unlimited champagne, laughing with the others at the witty toasts until it was time to cut the cake, Ben's hand warm and firm as it guided hers. When the festivities were in full swing Ben whispered in Verity's ear that it was time they changed, and ran with her up the broad staircase, kissing her swiftly outside the room where she was to dress.

'Get a move on, Mrs Dysart,' he ordered, smiling. 'We must be on our way—see you downstairs in ten minutes.'

Verity kissed him back and went into the room, smiling, her smile fading as she saw Gussie enthroned on the window seat as she closed the door.

'Martha told me which room you were using, so I slipped up here for a little chat, darling—just like old times.' Gussie smiled slowly, stretching like a cat as she got to her feet.

Verity took off her hat, laying it carefully on the bed. 'An unexpected pleasure, Gussie.'

'I used to know the house quite well in the old days, you know.' Gussie smiled slyly. 'Does Ben still sleep in that ridiculous monk's cell of a bedroom?'

'I wouldn't know,' said Verity shortly, and sat down at

the dressing-table to brush her hair, willing Gussie to leave her in peace.

'I must hand it to you, Verity, you're a fast worker.' Gussie shook her head reprovingly at Verity's reflection. 'There was I, laying my soul bare to you at the cottage one minute—and when we came back from Spain the first thing I heard was that somehow or other you'd persuaded Ben to marry *you*! Too slick for words, angel.'

Verity laid down her brush and turned to face the other girl.

'Gussie, if you have something to say, just say it,' she said tersely. 'Ben wants to be off in ten minutes.'

Gussie's eyes were blue pools of limpid innocence.

'I just came to wish you good luck, Mrs Dysart. God knows you'll need it.' Her smile turned to a sneer. 'Ben doesn't love *you*! It's me he wants—always has. But don't worry, darling, you'll provide the most marvellous cover for us—at least you'll never have to wonder where he is when he's not at home!'

It was like a bad dream. All Verity's most secret suspicions were crystallising into the honeyed malice dripping from Gussie's pink-tinted lips, but her face showed nothing but a casual impatience as she turned away.

'Right. If you've had your say perhaps you'll run along now. I must change.'

'Oh but I haven't.' Gussie sauntered to the door, then turned deliberately, smoothing a hand over her midriff. 'Don't you think Peter looks absolutely ecstatic today? Only this morning I told him I'm pregnant and of course the poor darling's over the moon—he imagines the baby's his. But you and I know better, don't we!' With a final smile of spiteful satisfaction she glided from the room, closing the door behind her with a triumphant finality.

Verity sat staring at her blank face in the mirror, her mind refusing to accept the enormity of Gussie's implication. Listlessly she got up and took off her wedding dress and hung it up automatically, then subsided in front of the mirror, her reflected face white above the coffee satin of her slip.

It was silly to be so stunned, she knew, nevertheless she felt as though the ground had been cut from beneath her feet. She had thought Ben might be seeing Gussie occasionally, but for some reason her imaginings had never gone beyond that point. Gussie's barbed little announcement made everything suddenly sordid and shoddy, and Verity shivered, feeling as though some of the shoddiness were rubbing off on her own relationship with Ben.

She jumped, startled, as her mother swept into the room, scolding.

'Come on, love. Ben's already down there asking where you are. You'll be late, not to mention cold, sitting there like that.'

Obediently Verity slid into the new saffron silk shirt, her fingers clumsy with the covered buttons and the zip of her sepia tweed skirt. Hannah held out shoes and gloves, found the matching bag, and held the jacket for Verity to put it on, then stood back to look at the finished result, her eyes wet.

'Damn—my mascara will run. Be happy, babe. Remember it takes two of you to make a marriage, so do your best with your bit.'

Verity smiled shakily, her own eyes misty, and returned her mother's hug.

'Look what an example I've had!'

Ben was waiting at the foot of the stairs as she went down with a bright smile on her face to run the gauntlet of waiting guests with his arm through hers, cameras clicking as they entered the waiting Morgan. Verity had a confused impression of Ben's parents and her own, their faces happy and fond as they waved the pair off to a secret destination, Gussie's face just beyond them, like the cat who's swallowed the cream, her eyes gloating among the crowd. A faint shudder ran through Verity.

'Cold?' Ben put out a hand to touch hers.

'No.' Verity shook her head, determined to behave normally. 'As you've kept the honeymoon secret even from me am I allowed to know where we're going now we're on our way? Is it a long journey—do we have to catch a plane? I packed the sort of clothes you suggested.'

Ben laughed as the car reached the main road. 'I hope you weren't hoping for something exotic. No plane necessary, I'm afraid—our destination is The Sun at Wychford, less than twenty miles away.'

Verity looked at him in surprise. 'Why all the secrecy then?'

'I had no intention of letting anyone know we'd be so close at hand, also I had no desire to travel hundreds of miles before I had you to myself, Mrs Dysart. Do I make myself plain?' His sidelong smile was deliberately explicit, so much so that Verity could feel her colour rising. 'Besides which it's a very attractive inn and does a roaring trade with the locals; always a good sign, and the landlord's wife prides herself on her cooking. I've booked two rooms looking out on the garden and trout stream at the back of the building.'

'Sounds lovely.' Or at least it would have done to any other newly married, dewy-eyed bride, thought Verity bleakly. But under the circumstances a busy hotel in London's West End would have been easier. Ten days in utter seclusion was likely to prove a strain, one way and another.

It should all have been so perfect. The Sun inn was centuries old, a long, low building with a thatched roof, innumerable small windows sending out beams of yellow light in welcome as Ben parked the car in the cobbled yard at the side. Even this early in the evening the place was already busy, many of the settles and tables in the lounge bar already filled as Verity watched Ben sign the register. A hefty young lad took their suitcases up the shallow staircase to a red-carpeted, uneven landing where he unlocked one of the doors at the far end. Ben gave him a generous tip, winning a

broad grin of thanks, as Verity looked round a cosy
sitting-room bright with chintz, a log fire burning in the
small fireplace, the only incongruity the television set in
the corner.

Ben opened an adjoining door and ushered Verity
into another room. A dark oak fourposter bed
dominated this apartment, holding her entire attention
for a moment or two before she noticed that all the
furniture looked like genuine antique pieces, including a
charming, skirted dressing-table set on a raised alcove
in the bay window overlooking the garden.

Ben put the luggage down on the rack at the end of
the bed.

'Well? Do you approve?'

Verity took off her gloves and jacket, smiling
brightly. 'Of course I do—it's a lovely room.'

He leaned against one of the bedposts, looking at her
thoughtfully. 'I did think to carry you over the
threshold, but something in your manner quashed the
impulse.'

'Just as well, our porter would have been embarrassed.' She pointed to another door. 'Where does that
lead?'

'Bathroom.'

'Good. I'll have a wash before dinner.'

Ben caught her wrist as she brushed past him.
'What's troubling you, Verity? What's wrong?'

'Nothing. It feels a little strange to share a room with
a man I suppose. I never have before.' She gave him a
glittering smile, her hazel eyes unnaturally bright.
'You'll have to make allowances, Ben.'

'I will, gladly. I just want to know what I'm making
allowances for!' He held her wrist fast, his face close to
hers. 'At the moment I feel more like a gaoler than a
bridegroom.'

'Nonsense.' Verity freed her hand and shut herself in
the bathroom, leaning against the door, her breathing
uneven. Her reflection in the mirror showed flushed
cheeks and over-bright eyes, but no trace of the despair

she felt inside, to her relief. She closed her eyes tightly. Gussie just had to be lying, she had to. Verity splashed water on her face, lingering as long as possible before returning to the bedroom to touch up her make-up. Ben was hanging up the last of his clothes in a big oak press.

'What time is dinner?' she asked.

'I said eightish.' He glanced at his watch. 'It's early yet, shall I order drinks up here or shall we go down to the bar?'

'Oh let's go down,' she said instantly, eager for noise and other people.

'Shouldn't you unpack first?' There was no mistaking the dryness in Ben's tone. 'I'd like a shave, too.'

'Fine! Of course.' Energetically Verity opened her suitcase and began hanging up skirts and dresses, and folding underwear into a drawer in the chest. 'Should I change, do you think?'

'You look beautiful just the way you are.'

Verity turned sharply to see if Ben was serious. He was. The word beautiful was intentional, as was obvious by the way he was looking at her, his eyes lingering longest where the heavy silk of her shirt outlined the curves of her breasts. As he returned to her face he frowned.

'Have I said something to offend you?'

'You used the word beautiful,' she said questioningly. 'You've never said that to me before.'

'I've never said it to any woman before, as far as I can remember.' His eyes challenged her, daring her to disbelieve him.

'How surprising.'

'The truth often is.'

They stood looking at each other in silence, then he strolled over to his case and took out a wet pack and went into the bathroom.

Verity mounted the three shallow steps to the dressing-table and switched on the little silk-shaded lamp to do her face, adding more shadow to her eyes than usual, darkening her lashes with an extra coat of mascara. Blusher was unnecessary, and after a touch of bronze lip gloss and a flick of the hair brush she was ready. She put on her jacket and wandered aimlessly into the other room, glancing along a row of books on a shelf near the fireplace. There were some newish paperbacks, and one or two old favourites, including *Far From the Madding Crowd* and *Villette*. Verity smiled wryly, thinking a bride should hardly be looking for bedtime reading, starting a little as she realised Ben was watching her from the doorway, a sardonic look on his face.

'Looking for ways to fill up your time?' The satire in his tone was evident as he added a couple of logs to the fire and replaced the old-fashioned guard.

'Not precisely. When you know me better you'll find I can't resist books, in any shape or form.'

'Time will remedy the deficits for us, Madame Wife.' He held open the door for her with a flourish. 'In the meantime let us eat, drink, and do our damndest to be merry.'

Verity felt a great deal better in the crowded, low-ceilinged bar. It was very full, obviously a popular place to eat, judging by the amount of people prepared to wait for a table in the dining room.

'Shouldn't we go in?' asked Verity.

Ben shook his head and accepted a menu from a pretty waitress as they sipped gin and tonics standing at the bar.

'Mrs Dalton, the landlady, knows this is a special occasion for us.'

Verity wasn't sure she liked the sound of that. 'I hope they don't play the Wedding March as we go in to dinner.'

Ben's eyebrows rose. 'You don't want people to know we're married?'

Verity shrugged. 'Married, yes. It's the newly-wed bit that's always so embarrassing, somehow.'

He finished his drink. 'Have another. Perhaps the gin will help with the embarrassment.'

Verity agreed so promptly there was a pronounced twist to Ben's wide mouth as he turned away to order.

'It's a very interesting menu for a country pub,' she commented, when he handed her the glass.

'Perhaps this might be a good moment to confess that I ordered the meal in advance, too,' he said with a grin.

'How organised of you.' Verity raised her glass in toast. 'Here's to your choice, I'm sure I'll enjoy it.'

Not long afterwards they were hurried off to the dining-room by the waitress with the news that their first course would arrive in five minutes exactly. A bottle of champagne stood ready in a silver bucket as they took their places in the atmospheric, raftered dining-room, where every table but their own was occupied. A few curious glances were directed at them as the landlady herself bore a tray to their table and served them in person with individual salmon soufflé mousses masked with lobster and prawn sauce.

'Sorry to rush you,' she said briskly, 'but you must eat it at once before it spoils. Enjoy your meal.'

They thanked her and obeyed her instructions, hardly saying a word as they quickly despatched the delicious feather-light concoction and washed it down with champagne.

'You were dead right,' said Verity with a sigh as she finished. 'Mrs Dalton's cooking is out of this world. Perhaps she might pass on a few tips.' To her relief the warmth and the food and the wine actually were mitigating the effects of Gussie's bombshell a little. She smiled a little, thinking that any respectably sensitive female would have been entirely without appetite under the circumstances, instead of eating like a horse.

'Why the Mona Lisa smile?' asked Ben softly, leaning towards her to refill her glass.

'A private joke.' She opened her eyes fully as they met his. 'Perhaps if I drink enough champagne I might even tell you about it later, but in the meantime what are we eating next?'

'Wait and see,' he said teasingly. 'And if champagne

is what you want there's another one on ice for us. I kept to the theme of celebration for choice of the wine.'

Verity smiled in approval, her eyes widening as the next course arrived. This was more substantial fare in the shape of thick slices of fillet steak sandwiched together with ham, onions and mushrooms, then wrapped in perfect puff pastry and baked to golden perfection.

'Boeuf en croute,' announced Ben.

Verity was too busy eating even to comment for a while.

'I hope you haven't ordered a dessert,' she said at last. 'Even I am beyond eating another bite.'

'Then have some champagne, and in a little while we'll have coffee.' Ben leaned back in his chair, his eyes on Verity's face as she laid down her knife and fork with a sigh. She drank thirstily and held out her glass for more champagne.

'I don't think I should be knocking this back as if it were lemonade,' she said doubtfully, 'but I feel extraordinarily thirsty.'

'It's hot in here. And as long as you don't sing lewd songs as you go upstairs no one will mind.' Ben grinned as she frowned at him suspiciously.

'Are you trying to get me drunk?' she demanded.

Ben shook his head. 'Not drunk. Less tense, perhaps. Earlier on you were wound up like a watch spring.'

She nodded. 'I know. I'm a little better now.'

'Why, Verity?' Ben leaned towards her, his face urgent. 'Are you nervous of me, for God's sake? I could understand it if—well, we had never had our experience at the cottage. But under the circumstances, I don't quite see what you have to fear. In fact, if you want I'll sleep on the sofa in the little sitting-room up there until you get more used to the idea of having me around.'

Verity's eyes widened in surprise. 'Would you really? How very forbearing. That's not precisely what's bothering me, though—I hope I wouldn't be so wet.' She hesitated, her eyes falling. 'Shall we say I had a little shock this afternoon, and am only now beginning to recover.'

'Tell me what happened——' Ben broke off as the coffee arrived. 'Brandy, Verity? Liqueur?'

'No thanks. I'll stick to the champagne, I think.' Verity drank her coffee while Ben had a quick word with the waitress, then held out her glass.

'I thought we might go up to our little sitting-room and finish off our drinks in peace up there,' he said smoothly. 'It's very full here tonight, and I gather they'd like our table if we've finished.'

'Of course.' The last thing Verity wanted was peace and privacy, but there seemed no way to object, so she got up obediently, allowing Ben to drape her jacket over her shoulders as they made their way through the bar to the stairs.

'I'll just hang up my jacket,' said Verity, when they reached their rooms. She lingered in the bedroom, combing her hair unnecessarily while Ben replenished the fire and the promised champagne arrived.

'You *do* intend to get me drunk,' said Verity as she sat in the armchair beside the blaze.

'I want you to tell me what happened this afternoon,' said Ben inexorably, 'and if champagne is the only way to get you to talk, then champagne it is.'

Not sure if she liked the sound of that Verity accepted the glass he gave her as if it were a potion he was administering.

'You won't like it,' she said, her eyes troubled.

'How can you know until you tell me?' he countered, and sat down opposite on the small sofa, his eyes fixed on her face.

'I know!' Verity drank a little of the champagne and stretched out in the chair, her eyes on the flickering logs. 'You see, Ben, if I were a heroine in a Victorian melodrama I would nurture this dreadful secret in my bosom to the grave. Unfortunately I am definitely not heroine material.'

'I don't agree,' he said quietly.

'Don't you? How sweet.' Verity sighed. 'Well, Ben, if you must know the truth, when you left me at the bedroom door to change after the wedding, who should be waiting for me but Augusta Middleton herself. In person.'

Ben's face stilled.

'I might have known——'

'She is really not at all pleased that you've married me, you know.' Verity was surprised to find how easy it was to tell him once she'd made a start, wondering if champagne was a form of truth drug. 'In fact she's hopping mad.'

Ben jumped to his feet, and stood looking down into the fire.

'I can't really see that our marriage is actually anything to do with Gussie,' he said harshly, his face averted.

'Perhaps it might be a good idea to tell *her* that. As far as she's concerned your marriage to me is purely a marvellous cover for your extra-curricular activities with her.' Verity stiffened as Ben swung round to stare at her with a look of blazing distaste.

'My what?' He pounced, pulling her to her feet and shaking her slightly. 'Explain.'

Abruptly Verity was as hotly angry as he. 'That's what the lady said! She was very explicit. She told me you didn't love me—I was aware of that, of course—and that you would always love her, would presumably carry on (I use the term deliberately) as you'd always done.' She winced as Ben's fingers cut into her arms through the thin sleeves.

'And you believed every word,' he said through his teeth, his eyes like black ice. Verity looked back at him squarely, her head thrown back in defiance.

'She was so convincing, Ben. Especially the Parthian shot she let fly as an exit line.' A shudder of distaste ran through her body. 'She's pregnant, she told me, and Peter's on cloud nine. Unfortunately for him, Gussie's inference was that the child was more likely to be yours. Could it be yours, Ben—could it?'

She held her breath as she watched the ice in his eyes melt to white-hot fury for an instant before they abruptly went blank, Ben's whole face immediately closed and withdrawn as the familiar shutters came down on his emotions. His hands dropped from hers and his body relaxed deliberately as he turned away. He leaned an elbow on the chimneypiece and resumed his inspection of the flames. When he finally spoke his voice was so conversational and matter-of-fact he could have been discussing the weather.

'If you consider a question like that necessary, Verity, what earthly point is there in any denial of mine? As far as you're concerned I seem to be tried and convicted in advance, so I shan't trouble myself with useless refutations.' He strolled over to the tray and took the bottle of champagne from its nest of ice, filling first her glass then his own. 'A toast, my trusting wife. To connubial bliss!'

Verity sat down in silence, sipping from her glass in sudden, cold sobriety. Her tension mounted as she watched Ben polish off the entire contents of the bottle in swift, quiet succession as she refused any more for herself. She felt shattered, and would have traded her immortal soul to take back her words. It was rapidly becoming obvious that Gussie's venom should have been put aside, ignored, never allowing her the triumph of engineering this disastrous start to the Dysarts' married life. So much for hindsight, she thought bitterly, looking across at Ben. He was lounging back on the sofa in apparent relaxation, his jacket and tie removed, the empty champagne flute suspended from one lax hand as it swung over the arm. Suddenly the silence seemed insupportable.

'Well?' she blurted. 'What do we do now?'

A thoroughly disquieting smile spread slowly over Ben's face as he replaced his glass on the tray with painstaking care.

'Do? For a lady of your intelligence that seems an excessively silly question.' With maddening deliberation he rose slowly to his feet and took the glass from her unwilling hand, finishing off the rest of her champagne before putting the glass on the tray. 'You obviously didn't want that—pity to waste vintage champagne. Now, what were we talking about?' He eyed her with a look of disquieting speculation. 'Ah yes, you were asking me what we should do next. What do you suggest? Perhaps you fancy Match of the Day, or one of those ancient black-and-white films they unearth for Saturday nights?'

Verity stared at him in stony silence. Ben gave a tigerish little smile and pounced suddenly, yanking her out of the chair.

'We are going to do what any other, normal, right-minded newly-weds would do at such a juncture, my beautiful bride. I shall now remove these elegant clothes and teach you that love—or what passes for it between you and me—is by no means all hearts and flowers; not by a long way. Pity really. Our wedding night would have been so much more romantic with a little trust and understanding, but never mind, we'll just have to do the best we can without it.' And his lips came down on hers, prising them apart in a cynical parody of his previous kisses.

There seemed little point in resisting. The arms holding Verity were vice-like in their grip, allowing her no movement of any kind, so she remained quiet in his grasp, letting him do what he wanted. He raised his head, looking down reflectively at her mutinous face.

'No response, Verity?'

'Only to remind you of your suggestion to sleep out here tonight,' she said calmly.

He smiled with hateful indulgence. 'Ah, but that was before I realised you knew the extent of my villainy, dear heart. Now you know what a blackguard I am what point is there in my trying to rise above it?'

Without warning he picked her up and strolled unhurriedly into the bedroom, kicking the door shut behind him. Verity remained impassive in his arms, knowing only too well there was no dignity or benefit in struggling. Her athleticism was no match for someone trained in armed combat, and she knew it. She lay flaccid and limp like a rag doll as Ben laid her on the bed and removed her clothes with a swift competence that was almost insultingly impersonal. Head averted she let him get on with it, shutting her eyes tightly, yet unable to control the little gasp of shock as he came down beside her, her eyes flying open to see his grin at her involuntary reaction to the contact of their naked bodies.

'Are those your tactics, my darling?' he asked caressingly. 'Just to lie there and think of England?'

Her eyes flashed at him like an angry cat for an instant before her lids dropped and she turned her head away, the endearment adding fuel to her fury.

'Not England,' she said sweetly, 'just Gussie.'

She had precious little breath to say anything for some time after that as he proceeded to render her helpless with pitiless expertise to the point where nothing existed but the terrible, beautiful sensations he was inducing with a concentrated violence that was almost detached. Without opening her eyes she knew he was watching her writhe and twist, his satisfaction complete as she moaned and pleaded, helpless in the grip of this purely physical cataclysm that engulfed her, the only sound he made the strangled sound in his throat as he finally became a victim of the same irresistible force. Then without a word Ben left her and went from the room. Verity put out an unsteady hand and switched off the light before sliding out of bed and stumbling to the bathroom in the dark, unable to face even her own reflection. She stayed there for several minutes, wishing she could lock herself in, but eventually she went back to the bedroom, fumbling in the chest for the sleek, satin nightdress bought in such naive anticipation for the occasion. She slid it over her head and climbed wearily into the bed, almost jumping out of her skin as two hard hands came out and pulled her against a warm, bare body.

'A waste of time, putting this on,' said Ben in her ear.

'I thought you'd gone to sleep in the other room,' she snapped, trying to wriggle away.

'Wishful thinking. I merely went to damp down the fire for the night. The fire in there I mean.' His voice roughened and he caught her hand to hold it against him. 'Not this one.'

Verity's face flamed in the darkness and she twisted away.

'Please, Ben. Don't. We'll both regret this——'

'I won't, I assure you.' At his husky little laugh she renewed her efforts to escape, but without much success, as her movements quite obviously gave him a great deal of unintended pleasure. Breathless, Verity struggled hard for some time, but it was a losing battle. She was fighting two opponents, Ben and her own body, and after a while she was forced to admit defeat. Far into the night he continued his demonstration of just how easy it was for the body to make love with a passionate intensity quite divorced from any feelings of the heart where he was concerned. For Verity, lying dry-eyed and wakeful in the darkness, it was very different. Her own heart, indifferent to Gussie and her revelations, was deeply and irrevocably involved, its commitment more, not less complete following Ben's prolonged, relentless possession. It was not a thought that brought her comfort.

CHAPTER TEN

VERITY clutched her cup in both hands, glad of the warmth as she sipped the steaming coffee. The morning was cold, and she shivered as she stared out into the bare, December garden. Very little of it was visible. An eerie, chill fog hid the river and was beginning a tentative advance towards the house, tentacles snaking out to loop the branches of the willows and writhe upwards over the lawn. Turning her back on it Verity tightened the sash of her velvet robe and went to fetch the mail and the morning paper. There were only a few circulars, addressed to Ben, and she left them beside a bowl of rust-red chrysanthemums on the hall table, catching sight of her pale reflection in the oval mirror above it, wraith-like against the vivid red of her robe and the flowers. Positively gothic, she thought, noting with distaste the dark shadows under her eyes before glancing up to see Ben coming downstairs dressed in a heavy tweed suit, his sheepskin jacket over one arm.

'Good morning,' she said coolly, and went back to the kitchen.

Ben followed her, frowning. 'It wasn't necessary for you to get up too.'

'I need to drive over to Temple Priors early today— with you and your father away there's a lot to see to.' She looked at his shuttered face in polite enquiry. 'I thought you might like a cooked breakfast before the journey.'

He shook his head. 'No thanks. Just coffee.'

Verity poured it, black and sugarless, and handed the cup to him.

'Perhaps if you cut down your consumption of Scotch at night you might find the thought of breakfast easier to contemplate,' she said dispassionately.

Ben scowled, looking at his watch as he swallowed the coffee hastily.

'If I drank less I'd sleep less, so give me leave to organise my own nocturnal arrangements.'

Verity shrugged indifferently. 'Of course. How long will you be in Scotland?'

'No idea. Up to Dad really—as long as it takes to buy this bull he wants, I suppose. I'll ring you.' Ben tugged on his coat and picked up his hold-all as a horn tooted faintly outside, the sound muffled by the fog. 'There he is. I'd better be on my way.' He hesitated, turning round to face Verity as she followed him to the door. 'Take care in this fog—why don't you stay up at the house with Mother?'

'She did ask me, but I'd rather sleep here.'

'Unwilling to leave your precious house for even a night?' Ben raised an eyebrow. 'You treat it like a lover.'

'I wouldn't know,' said Verity levelly. 'I've never had a lover.'

'And I thought you had. Just once, anyway.'

Verity ignored this. 'Goodbye, Ben—take care.'

To her surprise he bent and kissed her swiftly, then went through the door, swallowed up in the fog before he reached the bridge at the bottom of the garden. Verity shut the door thoughtfully, and went upstairs to dress, putting on heavy wool trousers and flannel shirt, a thick rollneck sweater on top to keep out the cold. Unlike Ben she was hungry as usual, and grilled herself some bacon and tomatoes, sitting down to eat them in comfort, the morning paper propped up against the percolator. Usually she liked to watch the bluetits and the nuthatches feeding from the wire container of nuts in the garden, but none of the birds seemed to know it was morning.

In some ways she was almost glad to be alone, grateful for a respite from this charade of marriage she and Ben were playing. Basically a straightforward girl, Verity was exhausted by the sheer necessity of always being on her guard with Ben, in public affectionate and devoted, in private civil and semi-detached. This double standard had been started in some ways on their brief honeymoon. By day Ben had driven her all over the Cotswolds, with occasional forays as far as Wales and the West country, taking her to every possible place of historical and geographical interest he could think of before driving back to Wychford for dinner each evening followed by hot, dark nights in the fourposter bed, where he taught her every last thing he knew about making love.

That, however, had been the only experience of 'connubial bliss' granted to Verity. On their arrival at Tern Cottage Ben had moved his belongings into the guest room and had remained there the entire four weeks and three days—and nights—since, leaving Verity to many a sleepless night in solitary state in the master bedroom. This morning had been the first intimation Ben had given that he had any similar problem with insomnia, and Verity felt distinctly cheered by the thought. Neither of them ever referred to the cause of their estrangement, and sometimes Verity wondered bleakly if Ben wanted a divorce, though determined never to bring up the subject in case he said yes. At first she had hoped fervently that their strange, angry honeymoon might have resulted in a baby, eventually glad when this hope was scotched. If she had a child she wanted one born of love, not resentment.

With more than enough time to herself to mull over Gussie's insinuations Verity reached the bitter conclusion that she had behaved like an idiot, playing right into Gussie's soft white hands. That lady's intention had been to ruin Verity's honeymoon as effectively as possible, even if it meant the end of any relationship she herself might have with Ben. With disgust Verity remembered Gussie's resentment in school on their final Speech Day. Verity had been awarded the Geography prize, and Gussie, who had always considered any form of study a waste of time, had been furious. The prize, an expensive Atlas, had suffered a mysterious accident a day or two later, a bottle of ink tipped over its centre pages, though Gussie had been hysterical with her denials of guilt. No doubt her motivation had been the same when she heard Ben was to marry Verity. It was hardly in her power to prevent the wedding, but skill in spoiling Verity's happiness in her marriage was well within her grasp. And if Verity had not been so consumed with jealousy and distaste she would have recognised Gussie's ploy for what it was.

Verity sighed. It was all very well to be so sane and sensible about the whole thing in retrospect, but the fact remained that she had voiced her suspicions to Ben, and he looked likely never to recover from the insult. She scowled as she cleared away her breakfast things, thinking Ben was behaving in a very stiff-necked way about the whole thing; after all, there was no denying that once upon a time he had been highly enamoured of the fair Augusta. Verity felt it would have required a nobler nature than hers not to need some reassurance in the face of Gussie's statement, whether it were true or not, and wondered how Ben would have reacted if the situation had been reversed. As she was never likely to know, she locked up the house and set off for Temple Priors in her Mini, sensibly deciding that work was the best antidote for her depression.

The day was unusually busy, with Ben and his father away, broken only by a very brief lunch with Isabel Dysart, who scolded Verity for working so hard.

'You work longer hours here for love than ever you did with Lockhart and Welch,' she said severely. 'Ben expects too much, Verity. I must have a word with him, you look very tired.'

Ben too, thought Verity privately. Their mutual insomnia was beginning to show.

'I enjoy the work,' she said reassuringly, 'really I do. There's not much to do at the cottage and I'm used to having plenty to occupy me.' She glanced over at the window in dismay as she caught sight of snowflakes beginning to come down thick and fast past the window. 'Oh no, Isabel, here we go again. A third fall of snow this early in the winter.'

'If it's like this here it must be worse in Scotland.' Lady Dysart looked anxious. 'I hope Hugh and Ben don't get stranded somewhere.'

'They were using a helicopter to get about up there, so don't worry, I'm sure they'll be fine.'

'Well *you* must stay here tonight,' said her mother-in-law. 'I really don't like to think of you alone in that cottage, especially in this weather.'

Verity shook her head and jumped to her feet, swallowing the last of her coffee. 'Thank you so much, but I think I should go home—I'm haunted by thoughts of burst pipes and water on the carpet. I'll get off before dark today, though.'

It actually was dark by the time Verity had trudged on foot down over the fields to the river through a thick layer of snow. When she got home she switched on all the lights and turned up the heating a couple of notches, then went upstairs for a bath and a change into warm pyjamas and Ben's wool dressing-gown, thick wool socks and furry slippers on her feet. She chuckled at her reflection in the hall mirror on her way to the kitchen. If someone broke in with pillage and rape in mind her appearance would be the only deterrent necessary.

Verity cooked herself a couple of cutlets and made a small salad, the radio on for company as usual. A news flash told her that severe weather was expected in the Midlands during the evening, with a gradual thaw overnight. Reassured she put her dinner on a tray and ate it in front of the television in the drawing-room, curled up on the sofa. Afterwards she inspected the weather now and again, but there seemed no let-up in the heavy white curtain falling steadily outside the window. Her mother-in-law rang a little later asking if Verity was all right, advising her to stay indoors the following day.

'Morrison can manage this end and I don't like the thought of you out and about in this weather. It's almost four miles up here by road, and it must be well over two if you come along the fields at the back, so have a lie-in for once and get some rest while Ben's away.'

Verity promised and rang off, smiling. Lady Dysart was plainly under the impression neither of them got much sleep under the same roof; which was true enough in its way, but not for the reason popularly believed. Almost immediately the phone rang again, Ben's clipped tones easily recognisable even above the crackling on the line.

'I rang before. The line was engaged.'

'Yes it was.'

'I know that—who was it?' he demanded.

'Your mother,' said Verity, irritated.

'I see. How's the weather down there?'

'Thick with snow, but a thaw promised overnight. How is it with you?'

'Pretty bad—it'll probably wash out the trip. I'll let you know.'

'Fine. Hotel good?'

'First class. Did you work today?'

'Yes. But I came home early when the snow started.'

'You should have stayed with Mother,' he said again.

'I'm afraid of burst pipes.'

'More than things that go bump in the night?'

'Much more.'

'I must go. Stay indoors tomorrow if the weather's bad. Goodnight, Verity.'

'Goodnight.'

Verity put down the telephone and stayed where she was for a moment, her eyes absent as she remembered the time when the terse, dictatorial voice of this evening had once murmured such erotic things in her ear down the line in what seemed like another existence. After a while she went to bed to watch the television Ben had bought for those 'sinful Sundays' that had never transpired. She was glad of its company as the old house settled down for the night, very much aware of creaks and groans never noticed when Ben was home. Drat Ben and his 'bumps in the night' she thought crossly and with determination settled herself for sleep. At some stage in the night she woke to the sound of wind and rain lashing against the windows and cuddled down relieved. The thaw had arrived.

Verity slept late the following morning, feeling absurdly guilty as she rolled out of bed, yawning widely. She drew back the bedroom curtains to stand aghast at the sight that met her eyes. Rain was driving against the glass, but it was still possible to see that the river had risen alarmingly. She dressed rapidly and flew to the landing window to look at the front garden, her eyes widening in concern as she saw the bridge was gone, obviously swept away by the debris rushing past in the swollen river. She ran downstairs to collect anorak and rubber boots, then went down the back lawn and along the bank to the other bridge among the willows. She stopped short, hands in pockets as she stood in the freezing, drenching rain, staring at the place where the bridge had been, coming to terms with the fact that she was cut off until the water went down, unless she wanted to swim the river. Shuddering at the mere thought Verity went back to the house to ring Lady Dysart and explain the situation, but discouraged any idea of someone being sent to help.

'Frankly I don't think there's anything anyone can do at the moment, Isabel, and the men have enough to cope with as it is. It isn't as if I'm in any danger, really.'

'But my dear, aren't you a bit apprehensive?' Isabel Dysart was obviously worried.

'Not in the least,' said Verity stoutly. 'I'll soon call for help if I need it, and the water's bound to stop rising soon.'

'Do you have enough to eat, Verity?'

'Masses of food. Enough for a siege. Don't worry, please, I'm fine.'

Despite her brave words, Verity was seized by a deep longing for Ben's authoritative presence. Nevertheless her optimism lasted fairly well through the hours of daylight. She occupied some of the time in making a meat pie and a couple of savoury quiches from recipes in one of the cook books received as wedding presents, and the highly successful results of her labours were cooling appetisingly on one of the counters when the radio suddenly went dead. Verity frowned, then switched on one of the lights. Nothing. Biting her lip she went to look out of the back window. The river was now past the willows and encroaching on the lawn. It was deadly quiet without the radio until inspiration struck. One of the drawers in the kitchen unit was given over to Ben's possessions, and to Verity's jubilation it contained a whole beautiful box of transistor batteries, not to mention a couple of dozen candles. Once the radio was functioning again and several candles were installed in pottery soup bowls Verity felt very much better, and decided it might be a good thing to inform someone she was without light. The telephone, however, also proved to be dead. Verity grinned ruefully; elements two, manmade miracles nil she thought, and took stock of her situation. The refrigerator was full of things like bacon and eggs, that were no use without some means of cooking them, but it also contained a couple of pints of milk, yoghurt, salad ingredients, ham, cheese, butter and orange-juice. The food in the freezer would last for a couple of days as long as she kept it closed as much as possible, but she would need bread. Verity whipped two loaves out of the freezer at once, then stopped dead, a loaf in each hand in the shadowy room as a thump came against the front door.

'Who—who is it?' she called, her voice an undignified squeak. There was no answer except for another muffled thud. The gloom in the hall was sepulchral as Verity crept across it, her heart pounding as the thump sounded again. Shades of *The Monkey's Paw*, she thought with a shiver, then pulled herself together and marched over to the door, throwing it open to stumble over a very large, very wet yellow labrador, who shook himself all over her making graphic noises plainly intended to explain his plight. Verity made a tremendous fuss of him. She laid down newspapers in the hall and fetched candles, towel and brush and dried and groomed the grateful animal, who wagged his tail in constant appreciation. She examined his name tag by the light of a candle.

'It just says "Taff" and your telephone number,' she told him, grinning as he pricked up his ears at the sound of his name. 'I bet someone's in a terrible state thinking you're drowned or lost. Never mind. We have light, we have music—you'll like that if you're Welsh— and now let's see what we can find in the way of food for you.'

Verity opened a tin of corned beef, mixed it with crumbled water biscuits and put it down on an old plate on the kitchen floor, then mixed dried milk and water in a plastic bowl and gave Taff that too, the whole lot disappearing like magic.

'Come on, let's go for a quick walk,' she said briskly, 'I'd like to keep an eye on that river.' She felt a great deal more cheerful now she had the dog for company, her spirits raised even further when she found a black rubber-covered torch at the back of Ben's drawer while searching for a length of cord to tether Taff in place of a lead. Even with the help of the torch it was difficult to tell what the water was doing in the darkness, but the rain was still streaming down, it was decidedly chilly, and Verity felt ready to sell her soul for a cup of hot coffee. As she and Taff went past the outhouse she had a thought. Nick's camping equipment was stored in there and it was just possible there might be something to cook with among it. With the dog sniffing round in great interest Verity shone the torch round the shadows of the outbuilding, giving a war-whoop of joy as the beam picked out a camping stove and several container of gas.

'Thank you, Nick,' she said with gratitude, and bore her trophies into the house with triumph, the dog close at her heels.

While a pan of water came to the boil on the small stove Taff was subjected to another rub down, then Verity made herself the desired coffee, drinking it with relish, and sharing the biscuits she ate with Taff, while she considered the unthinkable prospect of water on her beloved Shiraz carpet if the house actually were flooded. The idea nagged like toothache, and eventually she went into the drawing-room, running her hand through her dishevelled hair as she considered the best way to deal with it. She pulled the chairs and table away and rolled the freed carpet laboriously, then inch by painful inch she dragged it out of the drawing-room and up the stairs, not daring to pause in case the whole thing slithered down again. Halfway up the flight she began to regret the entire idea bitterly, especially as the dog thought it was some kind of game and barked with enthusiasm, licking her face now and then whenever he could reach it. Verity was very glad when the carpet finally came to rest on the landing and so could she, collapsing in a heap with the dog, her heart going like a trip-hammer and her breath labouring in her chest. She froze as she realised the hammering was coming from the front door, as well as her heart. The dog snarled, the fur rising on his back as he sensed her fear, the hammering beginning again as she crept warily down the stairs.

'Verity!' roared Ben's voice. 'Let me in, for God's sake.'

A great tide of relief rendered Verity almost limp as she reaced to the door and unbolted it, throwing it open to the sodden man who catapulted into the hall to be greeted with frantic barks from the excited dog, who was obviously prepared to do his best to defend Verity from all comers.

'Where the hell did *he* come from?' demanded Ben, who was shaking the water from his dripping hair in much the same way as the dog had done earlier. Verity flew to the cloakroom for a towel, and Ben rubbed himself energetically in the flickering light.

'Thank God you've got here—how did you manage it——' Verity took a good look at him to find he was naked except for a pair of brief navy underpants. 'Good grief, Ben, you'll get pneumonia——'

'Like Leander, I sort of swam the Hellespont, or was it some other chap,' he said, his teeth chattering as he tried to grin. 'Give me the torch, explanations later, I'm going up to find some clothes.'

'The water in the tank might still be warmish,' said Verity anxiously as he ran upstairs. 'You'll have to rub yourself down well afterwards——' she broke off, giggling at his colourful language as he tripped over the carpet.

'What the blazes have you been doing?' he bellowed. 'It's like an obstacle course up here.'

'Never mind that now,' she shouted, and lit the camping stove. 'Get a move on.'

She put a pan of water to boil then flew into the drawing-room with the best part of a box of firelighters, stuffing them under the piled logs with prodigal extravagance, and soon had a steady blaze which gave the added bonus of light as well as warmth. Ben came in shortly after, rubbing at his hair, and dressed in a dark roll-neck sweater and some ancient military-looking trousers with a large pocket on one thigh.

'What happened to the carpet?' he asked.

'Nothing. I was worried the river might rise up as far as the house, so I dragged the carpet upstairs.' Verity sat back on her heels, suddenly conscious of a shiny nose and wildly untidy hair. 'I'm a bit of a mess, I'm afraid. Sorry to be at such sixes and sevens—I wasn't quite sure what to do for the best.'

Ben grinned down at her, the flames flickering on his face as he bent down to help her up.

'I don't see how you can say that. I raced here in the Landrover to succour a damsel in distress, only to find you about as helpless as a Marine. I don't suppose all this hyper-efficiency would run to a spot of sustenance?'

'Of course.' Verity gave him a smug little smile as she hurried off to the kitchen and made coffee with the water bubbling away on the camping stove, handing Ben a steaming mug as he leaned against the counter-top watching her. He drank gratefully, his hand stroking Taff's head, the dog apparently reconciled to the intruder's right to be in the house.

'Where did this chap come from?' Ben asked.

Verity opened a tin of soup and poured it into a saucepan to heat, stirring it as she spoke.

'He arrived in somewhat similar fashion to you—soaked to the skin and thumping on the door for admittance. Must have got lost.' Verity smiled as she looked up from her stirring. 'At least he kept his coat on! Where are your clothes?'

'I parked the Landrover at the Bell when I saw you were awash. Stan Mayhew's lad came down the hill with me and took back the clothes I stripped off to swim the river. It's a bit deep by this time, and hellish cold, not to mention all the debris bobbing about in it.' Ben gave a reminiscent shiver and took a mouthful of the mug of soup Verity gave him.

'What a day!' Verity shook her head and cut a large slice of meat pie. 'I'm very glad you got home so quickly, Ben—I wasn't relishing the prospect of a night alone here by candlelight—even with Taff here to keep me company.'

'Nice to know I'm welcome.' Ben strolled over to the sink with his empty mug.

Verity eyed him warily as she cut some thick slices of bread and buttered them, but the flickering, dim light hid his expression. In the worn, functional clothes he looked tough and somewhat unapproachable, but there was no hostility in his manner as he asked what he could do to help.

'Nothing. It's not exactly exciting, but luckily I did some baking this afternoon to pass the time, so there's meat pie and some salad. No unnecessary plates as hot water's a slight problem.' Verity put the plate of food in front of Ben at the table, and sat down to join him, appropriating one of his hunks of bread to eat with a piece of cheese.

'God this tastes good,' he said, mouth full. 'This pie is first-rate—my compliments.'

'Thank you.' Verity felt absurdly pleased as she rose to make Ben some coffee.

'I rang you from Birmingham airport to say we were back, but of course I couldn't get through,' Ben said. 'So I drove Dad home first, heard Mother's frantic outpourings about the water rising down here and told her I'd see to everything and she could stop worrying.'

'It's very sweet of her. There was no way of letting her know I was all right unfortunately.'

'I never doubted for a moment that you'd cope,' said Ben matter-of-factly.

'No.' Verity sighed, then smiled cheerfully. 'It's always seemed much more logical to me to get on with things rather than flap about and wait for someone else to do them.'

'And quite right too.' Ben patted her hand and drained the last of his coffee. 'Thank God for practicality or I'd still be starving—I presume that's poor old Nick's stove you found?'

Verity nodded and cleared away the dishes. 'Once I had Taff for company I was braver about poking about out there in the dark. Would you see to the fire while I wash these?'

Ben saluted solemnly and went off to pile more logs on the fire in the drawing-room while Verity tidied up. She thought half-heartedly about going upstairs to make some repairs to hair and face, but decided not to bother. In the dim light her shiny nose and untidy hair would go unnoticed, and her black wool trousers and cream-and-grey Fair Isle sweater were as attractive and

practical as anything she owned, added to which she felt
suddenly weary. The mental and physical demands of
the day suddenly hit her as she joined Ben and the dog
in front of the leaping flames. Ben stood back in
satisfaction as the last log caught, glancing down at
Verity as she curled up on the settee with a sigh of
satisfaction.

'Tired?'

'A bit—and happy to be able to relax.' She scratched
Taff's head contentedly. 'If you hadn't arrived I wasn't
going to bother with lighting the fire.'

'Why not?'

'My plan was a thermos of coffee, a couple of hot
water bottles to take up to bed and a read by
candlelight huddled under the duvet.'

'My arrival seems to have spoiled your cosy little
programme,' Ben said without expression, and sat
beside her.

'Quite the reverse. I was never so glad to see anyone
in my whole life,' said Verity candidly, too tired to
bother with evasion.

There was a companionable silence for a while,
broken only by the crackling of the fire and an
occasional snore from Taff, who was stretched out in
abandon to the warmth.

'I think I'll take a look outside and see what the
river's doing,' said Ben eventually with a yawn. 'This
chap had better take a walk too. Come on. Here, boy.'

Verity lay full length after the dog followed Ben
outside, her eyes hypnotised by the leaping flames,
wondering how Ben had taken her remark, but too
warm and comfortable to worry much. Wrestling with
the elements was inclined to reduce personal differences
to size, altering the perspective considerably. When Ben
came back into the room he was alone.

'Where's our furry friend?' asked Verity.

'I've settled him on the rug under the kitchen table
and told him that's his bed,' said Ben, smiling. 'Want a
drink?'

'M'm, please. Anything.' Verity sipped the brandy and ginger ale he handed her, swinging her legs to the floor to make room for Ben as he returned with a glass of whisky and sat down with a sigh.

'I must be out of condition,' he said in disgust.

'No wonder—skinny-dipping in this weather! I only hope you don't get a cold, or worse.'

Ben drank half the whisky in one swallow.

'Not very likely. I've weathered worse conditions than these. But I was worried, to say the least. Mother was in a bit of state when I arrived, as she knew the river was rising, and with no power and no phone she thought you might be terrified.' He glanced sideways at her. 'Were you?'

'Not terrified exactly,' she answered thoughtfully. 'I was more concerned with possible damage to the house, I suppose——'

'Needless to say!' Ben's teeth glinted in the firelight, but Verity refused to rise.

'I must admit I wasn't very happy without light, but once I had the candles lit, and batteries in the radio I was better, and then Taff arrived, which made an amazing difference.'

'And then I came,' he said quietly.

Verity turned her eyes to meet Ben's. 'Yes. That was best of all.'

'You say that as though you mean it.'

Verity finished her drink and handed him the glass. 'I do.'

Ben rose and put their glasses on the silver tray on the cabinet.

'I thought I was permanently cast as villain of the piece.' He kept his back turned, apparently intent on pouring another drink. 'Would you like another?'

'No, thank you.' Verity eyed him in exasperation as he sat down again. 'Sometimes talking to you is virtually impossible, Ben Dysart. With that poker-face of yours it's heard to tell whether you feel pleased, or angry, or whatever. I said I was glad when you came and I meant it.'

'Presumably any human being to arrive at that point would have merited the same welcome,' he said dryly.

Verity gave up, and curled up into the corner of the settee, her head on a cushion. 'Of course, Ben. There must be dozens of people only too delighted to strip and swim a freezing river to my rescue. You just happened to get here first!' From the corner of her eye she saw him frown and put down his empty glass.

'I've had about as much as I can take,' he said abruptly, turning towards her. 'Look at me Verity.'

Verity looked, but said nothing.

'I swore I'd never say this,' he said huskily, 'but these last weeks have been purgatory. I've had enough.'

Her chin lifted. 'I have too. Do you want a divorce?'

'No I do not,' he said, glaring at her. 'Do you?'

She shook her head mutely. 'Then why have we been living in such bloody stupid misery?' he bit out, then checked himself at the mutiny in her eyes, breathing deeply as he began again with as much patience as he could muster. 'I have never seen Gussie alone since the day she met me in town to give me the original deed to Tern Cottage; about a week or so before the wedding.'

Verity stiffened, her eyes narrowing. 'You had lunch together.'

'No. Just a cup of coffee. She insisted. I was taking Mother in to town to do some shopping anyway, so I agreed to see Gussie for a few minutes when she rang to say Peter had turned up the original sixteenth-century document. You were out on an evaluation job somewhere.'

'No. I wasn't. It was postponed. I saw you with Gussie at the restaurant,' said Verity without inflection.

He looked at her in disbelief. 'Why didn't you mention it?'

'Why didn't you?'

'As the mere thought of Gussie seemed to cause trouble I didn't bother.' Ben sighed heavily. 'And so this is when you thought Gussie and I were cooking up our little plan for extra-marital fun and games behind our respective partners' backs.'

'It wasn't even that idea that made me cringe,' said Verity, with truth. 'It was the thought of both you and Peter Middleton as co-fathers to Gussie's offspring.'

Ben's facial control deserted him completely, his face rigid with distaste at her words.

'Any child of Gussie's was fathered by Peter Middleton—at least, for his sake I sincerely hope so,' he said with emphasis. 'In any event, *not* by me. I thought I told you once—other people's wives aren't my scene.'

'Perhaps the circumstances of our first meeting were somewhat to blame for my misapprehension on the subject.' Verity fought down the hostility she had vowed never to show again. 'What sticks in my throat, Ben, is that you couldn't just say all this on our wedding night!'

'It was like a punch in the stomach.' Ben moved restlessly to the fireplace, kicking a log back into place. 'I was hurt and disgusted, and just plain bloody-minded, I suppose. The fact that you could even wonder if Gussie's story was true knocked me for six.'

'I'm just like anyone else, Ben, a human being who needs reassurance. No one knew better than I you were in love with Gussie once, and I needed you to say it was all over between you. I told you I was no heroine.' All at once Verity wanted nothing more in life than sleep, and she got wearily to her feet, not meeting Ben's eyes. 'I'm going to bed. As I said before, I'm glad you came. Let's leave the rest for the morning.'

'Yes, of course,' he said quietly. 'Off you go—I'll see to the fire.'

With a tired little nod Verity took one of the candles and went to pat the dog's head before she went upstairs. The bedroom was icy after the warmth of the drawing-room fire and Verity threw off her clothes at top speed, gasping as she washed hurriedly before diving into her bright red nightgown, glad of its high, frilly neck and long sleeves as she huddled, shivering, under the duvet

in the darkness. Her teeth were chattering so much they
drowned out Ben's footsteps on the stairs, and she
almost jumped out of her skin when he slid beneath the
covers and took her in his arms.

'Hello,' he whispered, and held her close.

'Hello,' she answered breathlessly.

'You forgot a hot water bottle, so I thought I'd
volunteer as substitute.'

Verity chuckled. 'The hot water bottle stays at my
feet.'

'Where I've been from the moment I met you,' he
said promptly.

'I bet you say that to all——'

'Wrong. Only to you.'

Verity lay very still, hardly daring to breathe.

'Do you want me to go now you're warmer?' he
asked softly after a while, his breath warm against her
ear. She shook her head silently, and they stayed quiet
for a long interval, his steady heartbeat solid and
comforting against her cheek.

'I've been a fool, Verity,' Ben said at last. His arms
tightened and she burrowed closer instinctively. 'Am I
forgiven for the way I treated you on our honeymoon?'

'If you mean the nights I must be honest—I rather
enjoyed them.'

He shook with laughter. 'You might have let me
know!'

'No fear. I wouldn't have given you the satisfaction!'

'Oh but you did, darling. Repeatedly!' Ben's voice
was hardly audible, but something in its cadence made
Verity's toes curl and colour rise in her cheeks.

'A good thing it's dark,' she said breathlessly. 'I'm
blushing. I probably match my nightgown!'

'Of which there is a great deal too much, for my
taste, regardless of colour.'

Verity pushed her hot face against his throat.

'This sounds silly, but I feel shy; stupid isn't it?'

Ben turned her face up to his and kissed her with a
tenderness that melted her diffidence instantly.

'No moonlight and magic tonight, nor the heat and skirmishing of our honeymoon. This is just how it should always be; the two of us together at the end of a tiring day. Am I making sense?'

'Yes, Ben.' Verity returned his kiss with warmth, but the old reservation still niggled at the back of her mind. He sensed it and held her away slightly.

'What is it? Tell me.'

This seemed the night for clearing the air, and Verity took the plunge. 'When you asked me to marry you liking and respect were the only emotions you seemed to consider necessary. Love was left out of it.'

'Pompous, stupid fool, wasn't I?' Ben kissed her lingeringly. 'I could no more help loving you than breathing, but it seemed too sudden to be credible—I thought you weren't ready for any declarations at the time.'

Verity could have hit him. 'You mean you've put me through all this grief and misery for nothing?'

'You seemed to believe Gussie, not me,' he said, frustrating her efforts to get free, 'which hardly provided an auspicious atmosphere for protestations of undying love—besides I was furious, as perhaps you noticed. Then when we came home I was disgusted with myself and thought I'd move into the other room until we got things on a more normal footing.'

'Only we never did,' murmured Verity.

'You were so remote and businesslike——'

'Hurt and miserable, you mean!'

Further argument stopped as Ben kissed her for some time, effectively banishing Verity's indignation, then he lifted his head a little.

'Do you love me, Verity?' he asked, his voice deadly serious.

'Of course I do,' she retorted impatiently. 'Why else do you think I married you?'

'I thought this house was the main attraction!'

'It helped.'

'We've been quite a pair of idiots, in one way and another,' he said huskily.

'*You* have.' She put up a hand to touch his face. 'And to put the record straight, you didn't really need Tern Cottage for bait, desirable property though it is—your best move was to turn up at the Conways in your gamekeeper rig. Very sexy.'

He gave a smothered laugh and bit her earlobe. 'So were you, with your blouse sliding off your shoulders and that silly mobcap on your head. I was bowled over completely.'

'You still haven't actually said the words,' Verity reminded him.

'What words?' he teased, and began kissing her all over her face. 'What do you want me to say? What more do you need to convince you? I bought a house for you, I've swum a river to come to your rescue— quite unnecessarily, as it happened, but the thought was there——'

'A lady likes a little verbal confirmation as well as action,' she said primly.

Suddenly Ben was serious. 'I've loved you almost from the beginning, Verity, and always shall.' His lips met hers hungrily, and she responded with such fervour there were no more words necessary, until minutes later he took his mouth from hers to whisper,

'Do you still need convincing?'

She slid her arms round his neck and brought his face down to hers.

'Yes, please, Ben. . . .'

Here's how to get this special offer from Harlequin!

OCTOBER
TREASURY EDITION
COUPON

As simple as 1...2...3!

1. Each month, save one Treasury Edition coupon from your favorite Romance or Presents novel.
2. In four months you'll have saved four Treasury Edition coupons (only one coupon per month allowed).
3. Then all you have to do is fill out and return the order form provided, along with the four Treasury Edition coupons required and $1.00 for postage and handling.

Mail to: Harlequin Reader Service

In the U.S.A.
2504 West Southern Ave.
Tempe, AZ 85282

In Canada
P.O. Box 2800, Postal Station A
5170 Yonge Street
Willowdale, Ont. M2N 6J3

RT1-C-2

Please send me my FREE copy of the Janet Dailey Treasury Edition. I have enclosed the four Treasury Edition coupons required and $1.00 for postage and handling along with this order form.

(Please Print)

NAME_____

ADDRESS_____

CITY_____

STATE/PROV._____ ZIP/POSTAL CODE_____

SIGNATURE_____

This offer is limited to one order per household.

SUPPLIES LIMITED

This special Janet Dailey offer expires January 1986.

HARLEQUIN

FIRST·CLASS

Sweepstakes

OFFICIAL RULES

1. NO PURCHASE NECESSARY. To enter, complete the official entry/order form. Be sure to indicate whether or not you wish to take advantage of our subscription offer.

2. Entry blanks have been preselected for the prizes offered. Your response will be checked to see if you are a winner. In the event that these preselected responses are not claimed, a random drawing will be held from all entries received to award not less than $150,000 in prizes. This is in addition to any free, surprise or mystery gifts which might be offered. Versions of this sweepstakes with different prizes will appear in Preview Service Mailings by Harlequin Books and their affiliates. Winners selected will receive the prize offered in their sweepstakes brochure.

3. This promotion is being conducted under the supervision of Marden-Kane, an independent judging organization. By entering the sweepstakes, each entrant accepts and agrees to be bound by these rules and the decisions of the judges, which shall be final and binding. Odds of winning in the random drawing are dependent upon the total number of entries received. Taxes, if any, are the sole responsibility of the prize winners. Prizes are nontransferable. All entries must be received by August 31, 1986.

4. The following prizes will be awarded:

   (1) Grand Prize: Rolls-Royce™ *or* $100,000 Cash!
   (Rolls-Royce being offered by permission of
   Rolls-Royce Motors Inc.)

   (1) Second Prize: A trip for two to Paris for 7 days/6 nights. Trip includes air transportation on the Concorde, hotel accommodations...PLUS...$5,000 spending money!

   (1) Third Prize: A luxurious Mink Coat!

5. This offer is open to residents of the U.S. and Canada, 18 years or older, except employees of Harlequin Books, its affiliates, subsidiaries, Marden-Kane and all other agencies and persons connected with conducting this sweepstakes. All Federal, State and local laws apply. Void in the province of Quebec and wherever prohibited or restricted by law. Winners will be notified by mail and may be required to execute an affidavit of eligibility and release, which must be returned within 14 days after notification. Canadian winners will be required to answer a skill-testing question. Winners consent to the use of their name, photograph and/or likeness for advertising and publicity purposes in conjunction with this and similar promotions without additional compensation. One prize per family or household.

6. For a list of our most current prize winners, send a stamped, self-addressed envelope to: WINNERS LIST, c/o Marden-Kane, P.O. Box 10404, Long Island City, New York 11101

You're invited to accept 4 books and a surprise gift Free!

Acceptance Card

Mail to: **Harlequin Reader Service®**

In the U.S.
2504 West Southern Ave.
Tempe, AZ 85282

In Canada
P.O. Box 2800, Postal Station A
5170 Yonge Street
Willowdale, Ontario M2N 6J3

YES! Please send me 4 free Harlequin Romance® novels and my free surprise gift. Then send me 6 brand new novels every month as they come off the presses. Bill me at the low price of $1.65 each ($1.75 in Canada)—an 11% saving off the retail price. There are no shipping, handling or other hidden costs. There is no minimum number of books I must purchase. I can always return a shipment and cancel at any time. Even if I never buy another book from Harlequin, the 4 free novels and the surprise gift are mine to keep forever.

116 BPR-BPGE

Name	(PLEASE PRINT)

Address	Apt. No.

City	State/Prov.	Zip/Postal Code

This offer is limited to one order per household and not valid to present subscribers. Price is subject to change. ACR-SUB-1